Wildflower Summer

Alyssa J

Cover: Under Cover Designs

Editor: Danielle Polisseni of D.P. Editing

ISBN: 979-8-218-84060-0

Oakfield Publishing House

*To those who wake up one day and realize the dream
they chased no longer feels like home—
this is for you.*

*Be like a flower.
Survive the rain but use it to grow.*
-Darren Hardy

Chapter One

Before my alarm even goes off, I'm wide awake. Spending the next hour staring at my ceiling, I try to tell myself to ignore the unease that settles in my stomach. It's routine now—these early mornings spent wondering what's the worst that could happen if I didn't turn up for work.

So far, I haven't managed to think of a good reason not to keep going in. I'm still thinking about it when the alarm clock finally goes off. I sigh and push on with my daily, mundane routine.

There's no thought behind the motions now, moving around the room, making my bed and getting ready for the day.

In the shower, steam clings to the air while a silent attempt at self-encouragement echoes off the walls. Pretending the shower is something spiritual, cascading down my body, it washes away all my worries.

By the time the faucet shuts off, the heaviness has doubled. Worse than before stepping in. Worse than it has ever been. Today feels unbearable.

"Get it together, Alexis," I tell myself as I step out of my building. "This is a big day for you."

Of all the things I should be thinking about, quitting my job shouldn't be one of them. I've worked my entire life for the job I have. Enduring so much discrimination because too many people still cling to the idea that women can't make good architects.

Those who did think I made a good architect attributed it to my eye for design and not my smarts. They said it was just natural that I knew how to make a space feel homey, or whatever their requirement was.

And more often than not, they tried to make an interior decorator out of me.

I had suffered through all that and still came out on top, I reminded myself. This gloominess that I'm dealing with right now is not something that is going to last forever. I'm going to get through it just like I have gotten through every other hurdle thrown my way.

"You're late!" my boss tells me the second I make it into the office. Maybe today will be a lot harder to get through than I thought. I arrived on time, but the necessary people won't arrive for another hour; meanwhile, my boss acts as if I'm incompetent.

"Have you gone through the presentation?" he asks, turning to look at me when I take too long to reply.

Greg Jr. is an odd-looking man. It isn't that I have a problem with older men, it's just this particular one who is much more of an idiot compared to his father, the senior Greg. The way his left eyebrow hangs lower than the right. And the permanent snarl on his face. So not attractive at all.

I've been at Foster's Architect long enough to watch the transition of power go from father to son.

That's not saying that Greg Sr. is better than his son, but a side-by-side comparison will show that the older Greg knew what he wanted and how to get it. Junior has only a vague idea of what he wants, and he expects you to give it both in shape and reality.

It's just exhausting. Hearing him speak or even try to command a room is arduous.

"Did you not hear me?"

Pulled out of my haze and plastering a fake smile on my face. "I was just going through everything again. The presentation is ready, and we'll be sure to win them."

In the early days, when I started working with Greg Jr.—after his father had introduced him as his successor and the one to take over the company going forward—he had turned to me and told me that I would become their lead architect and work closely with his son.

Back then, the sudden promotion had been too shocking to fully process what was happening. It was years later, after the approval of my first three designs, the meaning of working closely with Greg Jr. became painfully clear.

He took credit for my first design. Talking a big game about how he got the inspiration and stayed up endless hours. An interview that I had to prepare him for, giving him words that I should've said myself.

It was office politics, according to everyone. I needed to prove that I could hand these things over so the company would consider me for bigger projects.

Then the second project happened, and I found out that they weren't asking the same ridiculous demands from my male counterparts. They were letting them take the credit for others' work, meaning mine. One of my superiors had tried to convince me that my work was better than the men, then proceeded to steal it.

I didn't care too much for that. In fact, I was pissed. I didn't work this hard or come this far to give glory to someone else.

With project three, I threatened to pull out of the deal alongside my designs if they didn't give me credit for it. At first, the company acted like they didn't care what happened.

I started applying to other companies then, hoping one of them would take a chance on me, and one of them did. That's when Foster's Architect decided to not only give me credit for my work but also double my salary.

An incentive to make me stay.

The only condition then was to credit him as my assistant whenever my project was approved. It didn't matter to me as long as I was given credit for my work. So, I agreed.

If I knew that Greg Jr. would continue to be infuriating, I would have never agreed to those terms.

"You know how big this project is. You need to present it well; the design is really good, but you've never been good at presenting. I'll do it myself, but you've been the one in charge of all of this."

"I understand," I say, even if I really don't understand why they're making me do anything. I am making a lot of money, more money than I know what to do with. But this job has taken a lot from me mentally.

I work a lot—*too much*—and haven't managed to keep any close friends. No one that I can call on the phone and talk to about all that is bothering me. No personal life to speak of. No relationship that's lasted.

Breathing in slowly before exhaling, my gaze shifts from the man in front of me to the floor-to-ceiling windows on the left. When this office was first offered, that window had been one more incentive to stay.

When things get really tough, I stand by the window and stare down at all the moving vehicles, listening to all the rumbling and honking, wondering if anyone else is having as shitty a day as I am.

Now the only issue is, getting up and calming myself, but I can't. My boss seems to think that he's saying something life-changing to me, and I'm trying to make this worthwhile, but I really don't want to deal with it anymore.

"I quit."

Greg Jr. abruptly stopped talking. Now looking at me with his mouth slightly open and eyebrows raised high. "What?!"

"I quit," nodding my head this time, feeling all the weight I've been carrying on my shoulders lessen. It isn't all gone, but somehow, I feel lighter than when I came in this morning.

"You can't quit," Greg Jr. says with a roll of his eyes. "We have big clients coming today, Alexis. We're proposing the design for the new museum that the city is trying to build, and you want to do what? Walk away from it?"

"I don't want to do this anymore."

"Is this you asking for an increase in pay? You know, you can just ask and I'll take it up with the board. You can't threaten to quit every time you want a pay raise. It's the only trick in your book, and it's starting to get old."

I don't point out that every time I've gotten a raise in my salary, they were the ones who kept offering more money. Not once have I asked for an increase in salary; they just keep giving it to me.

But now, all the money in the world isn't going to convince me to stay. I'm done with the company, and I'm going to take a little break to figure out what I truly want or even need.

"I'm tired of working here and the way you all treat me," I tell him and get to my feet. I turn my computer to face my boss. "This is the presentation; if you can do it, fine and good. I don't want to do it, but since the design has already been done, you can go ahead and use it. I just want the credit for it. All the interviews and whatever comes from it, you can keep it. I just want what will come from letting us use the design."

"You're joking." Greg Jr. gets to his feet now. "You can't just leave; the clients are going to be here any moment. What do you want me to tell them?"

Shrugging my shoulders, I pick up my bag, put on my coat and turn to face my boss. Former boss. I smile at him; the first real smile I've given him since he was first introduced to me.

His face is red and twisted into something even more unattractive than it usually is. That is the thing with Greg Jr.; he always wears his emotions on his face. He never knows how to hide a single thing he feels. It's one of the things that makes him so unbearable.

"I'm certain you'll figure something out. You're a smart man."

Greg Jr. follows me to the elevator, yelling at the top of his lungs which draws the attention of all the other staff members.

"You can't just up and leave us right in the middle of all of this."

"It's not like I'm leaving you unprepared. And like you usually say, I do exactly what someone else can do. It's not like I'm leaving you short-staffed or anything like that. I am leaving you with the opportunity to take charge and give the task to someone who will do it more than I ever will."

I can't say where all this confidence is coming from, but now that I'm standing up to Greg Jr., I'm realizing that there's so much relief in doing so. It's such a shame that this feeling is coming at the expense of my job, but I'm sick and tired. Sick of being miserable and depressed. And just tired. For once, it's time I put myself first.

There are a lot of things I'm willing to die for, but this job, this city that's drained me, taking too much from me in exchange for absolutely nothing, is absolutely not one of them.

The elevator comes to a stop, and when it slides open, I nearly laugh from the coincidence of it all.

The clients stand in front of me, with a confused look on their faces. Today was supposed to be our first meeting with them, but that reality is now not going to happen.

They keep their eyes on me, then look past me to the man who I'm certain is completely red in the face.

"Gentlemen," I say by way of greeting, moving to the side to allow them to walk past.

"Alexis," Greg Jr.'s last attempt at stopping me, is a whisper and a weak tug on my shirt. I don't relent, stepping into the elevator with a smirk on my face. The last look I get of Greg Jr. is him taking his eyeglasses off and wiping his face furiously with the handkerchief that always sits in his pocket.

"I'll send my resignation letter via email," are my last words to the man who made my life unbearable for too long.

Free at last.

Chapter Two

The thrill of leaving my job lasts about twenty minutes into my drive home. The realization of what I had done dawns on me the moment I put my car in park, and panic sets in.

I take a deep breath to calm myself.

You can do this, Alexis. You're great at what you do. You will succeed.

Even though I resigned at that moment, it wasn't something that came out of the blue. Over and over, I thought about leaving this job and what I would do after, where I would go.

All of those thoughts seem out of reach now. The air in the car fills my skin with goosebumps.

I shake myself out of that thought. This place isn't going to be enough for me; I need to get out of this city.

The plan in my head has always been simple.

1. Quit my job

2. Move back to Willow Falls

3.

I never got around to writing down what the third thing would be, but since one is already checked, there is no point waiting around.

Once getting into my apartment, I started to pack up my things. It took me the entire night, but I managed to get everything needed for this trip. The rest of my belongings, I figured packers could haul them to Willow Falls, or I will donate everything I can't bring. At this point though, I'm not even sure staying in Willow Falls is going to be a permanent thing. But I need an escape.

My parents will be surprised to see me, but I hope they'll understand why I couldn't stay at that job any longer. They will welcome me with open arms, it's just the nerves from this big change.

I haven't been home in such a long time; the last visit was six Christmases ago, before Greg Sr. gave way to Greg Jr. and the company started overworking us and approving all of my projects.

The last couple of years consisted of pulling all-nighters to complete sketches, running on coffee and little food. It's wild that I or anyone can make it this far working like that.

After a night of probably the best and longest sleep, I've had in a while, I relax until noon. Then, I load all the necessities in my car and head out on the road. I need to make a stop for gas and of course, coffee.

When I settle down in Willow Falls, I'll call my building manager to let her know my plans to move. I'll ask for her help in making sure the movers do exactly what is needed of them.

"Time to go home," I say as I pull out onto the road.

Eight hours later, I'm carefully pulling into my parents' driveway. My father's truck is nowhere in sight. Maybe he's out on a work run.

When my career started booming, I really tried to convince my father to stop working, hire help, slow down, let someone else carry that weight. But he refused. Something about how being idle would drive him crazy. It must run in our blood as I imagine I would've said the same thing.

It's getting dark out when I arrive, so I'm careful to turn off my headlights before they shine on the house. Stepping out of the car, I take a deep breath, grinning as I'm not hit with the smell of fuel. My ears and mind appreciate the silence. So different from city life, and definitely what is needed.

Even though they live up the road on a farm, I know that a lot of the neighbors are standing by their windows looking up here wondering who pulled in so late. The older neighbors might remember me or even recognize my car.

Willow Falls is the type of town where people can smell a change in the air. As a kid, I loved it. I felt safe everywhere because everyone was watching over us and nowhere was unsafe.

No tragedy has ever rocked this small town, and everyone is determined to keep it that way. It is the picture-perfect town you read about in books and dream about after.

The door swings open and startles me. I turn to see my mother stepping out of the house, wrapping her cardigan around her small frame. Her hair is scattered everywhere, and her glasses are sitting crookedly on her face.

"Lexie, is that you?" my mother asks, her small voice coming out even smaller.

Taking a deep breath and moving toward my mother, I wrap my arms around her and inhale her perfume. "I missed you so much, Mom."

My mom says nothing but continues holding me like she knows that I've been fighting demons. And I wonder if I'm touch-starved, given how hard I'm clinging to her hug.

I sniff, holding back the tears because the longer I stay in my mother's arms, the harder I want to cry, and I would like to be inside the warmth of the house before she or I break down.

I pull away from the hug, asking, "Where's dad?"

"He went drinking with his friends. Today's their cheat day or whatever they call it."

"And he left you home alone?"

Mom chuckles, directing me into the house. I hear the command even when my mother doesn't say it; my father is responsible for bringing in the luggage, even though I try.

"I leave him alone plenty, today's just one of the rare occasions where I'm on the receiving end of the treatment. Besides, my ladies want to meet all the time, and we have a lot to keep us busy. They, on the other hand, don't have much going for them."

"I quit my job," I blurt out the second the door shuts behind her.

My mother turns to me immediately, her brows raised high. No words are uttered as I'm pulled back into her arms. This time, I don't stop myself when the tears start to fall.

Chapter Three

I woke up feeling panicked, and yelled, "I'm late."

Searching around for my phone frantically, wondering why it didn't ring, when suddenly the situation dawns on me. I quit my job and I'm in Willow Falls. I take a deep breath and fall backward onto my pillow to lie for a few more minutes before heading downstairs.

Phew.

Nothing has changed much about my childhood home. The same pictures are still hanging on the walls. Some from my childhood, some from my graduation. There's one from prom, and I move closer to see it better. I'm wearing a long, beaded emerald green dress. The one I begged Mom to get for me. My hair is in curls, and I'm smiling at the camera. Grant Carter, the boy I used to have a major crush on, was my date.

Grant had asked me out to prom in the grandest way possible. It's cheesy to think about it now, but the truth was that Grant got the whole school in on asking me to be his date. A few weeks prior he had notes sent to me that needed to be decoded. It was fun, and cute.

It's crazy to think that in all my years in the city, the boy I used to sneak out to meet barely crossed my mind as soon as I left town and headed off to college.

But that would be a lie. We promised to try and stay in touch. But our budding romance stood no chance against the demands of college, and the calls and texts dwindled until there was nothing left.

I would like to say I've moved on, but now that I'm looking at this picture, realization sets in that I haven't been happy in a very long time. I don't even think I've been happy since the last time Grant and I spoke.

I pad down the hall to the kitchen to fix up a cup of coffee. The coffee maker I bought the last time I showed up for Christmas sits on the counter, beckoning me to use it. My father was a big fan of french press instant coffee, never quite seeing the need to buy beans and brew it when he could get one in an instant.

I had no choice but to settle for the same thing. Taking two scoops out of the tin, I pour, then press and make my way outside.

Last night, I fell asleep waiting for my father to get home while taking comfort in my mother's arms. I must have made it to my room before he got home.

Sipping my coffee on the front porch, I embrace the quite morning. It's still dark out, but the sun is peeking through the trees over the barn. I have no idea when

the day begins around here, but if I remember correctly, life in Willow Falls begins slowly.

People ease themselves into it. They don't wake up
in a panic, thinking they've missed their train, or feeling ill-prepared for a presentation they've spent weeks
getting ready for. I wonder if I'd be able to align myself
with the lifestyle of Willow Falls again.

The door opens, and I turn my head to find my father
looking down at me with a smile on his face.

"You're up early," he says and takes a seat next to me.

I lean into his embrace and accept the kiss he places
on my forehead. I soak up his scent and the warmth he
gives off. This man raised me with all he had, and I've
missed him so much.

"You have a late curfew these days huh?" I say, my
voice taking on a playful, accusatory tone.

"I was out with the boys. Something to keep us feeling youthful. And your mother didn't call to tell me
you were home, otherwise I would have come home
immediately."

I pull away from the hug to shake my head. "It's not
like I'm running away. I'll be here a while."

My father doesn't reply immediately, but from the
corner of my eyes, I see him nod his head like he's
taking in what I just said. Last night, my mother didn't
ask me many questions, she just held on to me as we
both cried.

I assume that's why my father is sitting next to me now, asking the questions my mother didn't get the chance to ask last night. I have no idea if it's all the years they've spent together, but my parents are in sync in a manner that fills me with longing.

I've seen them have full-length conversations with just eye contact. I've wanted that my whole life, a person who can understand me from just one look, someone I can lean on without worrying that I'm taking too much from them.

"Did something happen?" asks my dad.

"It just became too much. You know?" I don't think he knows, but my father nods like he does. "It had just been building up, and it finally spilled over. I just don't want to be there anymore. I didn't feel like myself there. I want to be able to enjoy my job, and I just didn't anymore."

My father nods again, more rapidly than the last one.

"I understand that. You're welcome here any time. You can stay however long you want, forever if you need. Your mother and I have been so worried about you, and it makes us happy that you came home to us when it became too much for you. The last time you came home, you were really down, and we tried everything we could to convince you to stay, but you were always busy working."

I nod my head because I remember it all too clearly. The rushed phone calls, the hurried goodbyes, the missed calls because I had a deadline to meet or because a project due date had been bumped up.

Sometimes, from fear of worrying them, I just chose not to interact with them. Once, my mother threatened to come over to see me, and I took that as the motivation needed to start calling them back.

Sunrise is emerging with an orange hue. Despite the beauty it beholds, I'm suddenly filled with anxiety. With every intention of starting over in my hometown, where do I even begin? I'm in my 30's, no husband, just quit my dream job, and most likely going to be staying with my parents for quite some time.

While Willow Falls isn't full of spiteful people, it is a small town. The thing with small towns is that everyone wants to be in everyone's business. Everyone wants to know the gossip.

"I'm back now," I say with a small smile on my face.

My father smiles back at me. "You have all the time in the world to figure it out, kiddo. I'm glad you're no longer overworking yourself."

He pulls me into another hug and gets to his feet. "You should head back inside; your mom will be up soon if she isn't already."

"Where are you off to?"

He smiles at me, feeling all too proud of himself. "I have a meeting in the town over. Some race thing, and they'd like to use some of our horses. I'd like to make sure that wherever they take the horses, the conditions are ideal. You know, some of us still have to go out there and grind." He says with a wink.

Then, as if it's the funniest thing he's ever said and heard, he throws his head back and lets out a loud laugh, staggering the rest of the way to his truck. I get to my feet to wave him goodbye, the coffee cup still in my hand. I don't bother taking a sip of it again, knowing it had gone lukewarm.

I head back into the house after I lose sight of his truck. My mother is coming down the steps by the time I finish dumping my cup of coffee into the sink.

"You're up early," my mother says, smiling.

"Routine," I reply with a shrug of my shoulders.

"How did you sleep, sweetie?"

"I slept fine. I was thinking of walking around today, seeing what's new here. Any changes I should know about?"

My mother laughs a little and shakes her head. "You haven't been here for a long while. Everything is going to look new to you. What would you like for breakfast?"

"I'm not really hungry."

My mother hums but pulls a pan out of the cupboard, and she can barely contain her smile when the waffle maker is whipped out. If my mother sees the grin on my face, she doesn't call attention to it. She keeps talking about all the ways I can spend the day. Some things never change though, and I will never turn down a good homemade waffle.

"Do you remember Josie? She's Minnie's daughter. She came back a while ago and opened a café. Until it opened, we didn't really know we had a lack of coffee problem in Willow Falls."

I raise a brow at my mom.

"Okay, but aside from you, nobody else called it. And now, we're all coffee addicts."

"I'll be sure to check it out. I've missed Josie and need to catch up with her. What else should I be on the lookout for?"

My mother shrugs her shoulders again. "I think you should just take it all in. You're not in a hurry to go back, right?"

"I'm not really sure of anything. I came back home with the intention to take a break, but I don't know if I'm going to go back. I don't think I want to, but all of my things are there, and it's just too soon to decide."

"You don't have to figure anything out right now. We're happy that you're back, and that is more than enough for us. Take time to rest, and who knows how things will go from there. But always remember, what you want is in one hand, and what you get is in the other."

Chapter Four

Finally leaving the house after my mother all but kicks me out. I kept saying I'd go but tried to make excuses to stay. The more I thought about leaving the comfort of the house, the higher my anxiety climbed.

I want to go to the barn and see how things are going, but my mother is convinced I'll only get in the way right now. Plus, I need to rest more before taking on some of the responsibilities on the farm.

Apparently collecting eggs is now considered a difficult task. Still, I step out of the house and prepare myself for all of the people I'll be saying hello to. The townspeople who will remember me and ask how I'm doing, or old classmates. I'm afraid of having no excuse to let everyone know why I'm back in town.

"They won't really care," my mother says. "They have their own lives to worry about." Walking down the porch steps, their barn cat is sitting there purring. I bend down to pet him and then get in my car to drive to town.

I remember things differently. Even though they have their own things to worry about, knowing that the folks of Willow Falls take all the chances they can to worry about someone else's business.

"It's what makes us family," my mother used to say when I was a child as she was shoving a dollar in my hand with a direct command to take Josie, the girl who would become my best friend in high school, to the mall for ice cream after Josie's father died.

Willow Falls is a comforting town but remembering that time I was dared to break into the convenience store gives me anxiety, especially if I run into those ladies who ran it back then. A very regrettable decision on my part, and everyone seemed to remember me for that.

A cool breeze blows past me and birds tweet in the air. I take a deep breath and shut my eyes, pausing on the street to let the warm afternoon sun hit my face. There are no horns honking, the air doesn't smell of anything foul. No one bumped into me and asked me to move out of the way. No one is yelling.

There is nothing but cool serenity, punctuated by laughter. This is the first time I've heard laughter that doesn't irritate me. And for someone who felt irritated at any given moment, that is saying a lot.

I continue walking, smiling at those who recognize me, giving a small wave as I pass by.

A lot of stores in town have undergone some renovation, like the barbershop. It has a new sign that is painted a cream color with a stencil of a man in black paint. I smile, remembering going there with my father whenever he needed a haircut.

"Alexis," the barber, Tom Dexter, calls out, and I wave at him, crossing the street to greet him properly.

"Hi Tom," I say, accepting a hug from him. He's aged a bit since the last time I saw him, he has more grey hair and he's starting to slouch. His son, Jeremy, wobbles out of the shop to greet me too. Like his father, he's wearing an apron with the same stenciled man.

Now that I'm looking at Jeremy, it's easy to tell who the stenciled man is.

"Ah, I see," I say, winking at Jeremy. "You finally fulfilled your dreams of becoming the shop's ambassador."

Jeremy grins and nods his head. "I knew you were interested in me. Who else would remember this? Say, how long are you in town for? I can show you all the new places you might miss otherwise."

He's four years younger than me, and I think it's so silly that he hasn't gotten over his crush on me. Most people would have given up and counted it amongst their losses, but not Jeremy Dexter. The boy with two first names.

"You should give that up already," I say while shaking my head.

"You know, one of these days, I'll get you to change your mind." Jeremy says with a big grin.

"Don't listen to him," his father says with a shake of his head. "Where are you off to?"

"Josie's," I say with a smile. "My mother says she runs the café. Sadly, we lost touch and I haven't seen her in forever, so this would be a nice chance to surprise her."

"That girl makes fantastic coffee," Tom says, and Jeremy nods in agreement.

"Say hello to Josie for me. And tell Ms. Baker not to sell off all the baked goods, I'll be coming by later to have some."

I must look confused because Jeremy adds, "Josie runs the store with her mom. You should have come back more often."

Even though his tone is not accusatory, I can't help but feel scolded. I bow my head and purse my lips.

"Again, don't listen to him," Tom says and shoves his son lightly. "If I weren't hell bent on having him take over the family business, he wouldn't have stepped back in here."

Jeremy doesn't deny it. He simply grins then winks at me. My chest relaxes considerably. "Don't forget to deliver my message."

The way he says it, in a suggestive tone, makes me shake my head at him. I might deliver his message, I might not. It depends on how I feel when I get to the café.

The truth is I can't remember how my relationship with Josie fizzled out. Everyone, including myself, thought we would be friends forever. We even applied to the same colleges, but somewhere along the way, after we got accepted into different schools, our relationship dwindled.

Now that I'm thinking about it, none of my relationships made it after I left. If you don't count my relationship with my parents, and that's solely because they are my parents. Ugh, I feel so guilty for not keeping in touch with everyone. Being back here is bringing up so many feelings.

The bell above the café door chimes softly as I push it open. Cool air hits my face and I smile a little, taking time to scan around the room for a familiar face. Having no way of telling how Josie will react to seeing me, I'm hoping the welcoming will be as warm as the ambience of this café. I do a double take, *does the sign out front say, "Josie's Cafe", does she own this?*

It's cozier than expected. Unlike the minimalist spaces I'm used to in the city. Those coffee shops are always painted in boring colors with barely any decor. Here, I'm greeted with a colorful space, full of greens and golds. The one wall is a bright orange with plants on a shelf. There are fairy lights running from one end of the room to the other. The tables are placed closer to each other, with two equally square chairs with what looks like such a comfortable cushion.

There's a centerpiece on each table, a vase of flowers—fresh by the looks of it—and a jar of water. The café is somewhat empty, with only two people I don't recognize sitting at the table closest to the window. They spare me a look before going back to their conversation.

When turning to the ordering area, a woman is standing there with her mouth slightly ajar. I smile as I walk over, placing my hand on the table, I lean forward, and wink.

"Long time no see."

Josie Baker snaps her mouth shut and hurries from behind the counter to tackle me into a hug.

My hug is immediate. Feeling ridiculous for even worrying about how Josie would receive me showing up here, because she is incapable of feeling ill towards another person. We stay like this for a while and hold each other with Josie's face buried in my neck.

When we pull away from each other, I'm still grinning, but Josie, having had her fill from hugging her old friend, hits me lightly on the shoulders.

"You went away with no word," Josie accuses, "I tried calling, but never got a call back. Who abandons their best friend like that? To make matters worse, we were never in Willow Falls at the same time. I always showed up before or after you were here, never during. I've missed you."

I clutched the spot on my shoulder, looking at Josie with a small pout on her lips. The truth is she remembers it a whole lot differently than I do, but that's not the only thing I've been wrong about. When I left town and visited once in a while, I always assumed Josie picked the times when she knew that I'd be unavailable. It made sense at the time given how I managed to run into most of our other classmates but never Josie.

"I got busy in the city," I say, not the entire truth, but the version of the truth that I'm used to telling.

Josie pauses her actions to look at me. "That's everyone's excuse. You were the only one that stopped coming home after a while."

The argument sits on the tip of my tongue, but I manage to swallow it back down. I could argue or blame it on my job, but I'm not trying to hide behind that anymore. I don't want my identity tied to my work. I need to do better.

My phone buzzes in my pocket the second I go to give a reply. I smile apologetically at Josie and pull the phone out of my pocket. Greg Jr.'s name flashes on my screen and I hold back a groan.

This isn't something I need to deal with right now, but I haven't sent my resignation letter yet, so in a way, I still work for the man. I step out of the café, telling Josie I'll be right back in.

I accept the call, and before I could say hello, "We thought about it, and we've decided a paid vacation is the best thing you need to get yourself sorted out."

"A paid vacation? What are you talking about?"

"Yes, we figured you've been working for a long time, and you must be exhausted, so we're going to let you take a paid vacation, but only after this deal is done. Six months if you want."

"You're going to let me take a six-month paid vacation?"

"Yes, and it is going to be an all expenses paid trip to whatever vacation spot you pick."

Of all the ways I've expected this to pan out, I didn't expect them to offer me all of this at any point in time.

"We need you to come back and explain the project and see it through completion."

"That's going to take forever, and I don't think I want to be around for that long. I need to take a break, and while all of this is lovely, I don't want to come back. I'm sorry I haven't sent the resignation letter, so it seems like I'm joking about it, but rest assured that you're going to get it before the end of today."

"What I'm saying, Alexis," Greg Jr. says, and I can hear the frustration in his voice, "is that we don't want to lose you. We need you to stay with us, and we're willing to do anything to keep you with us. Isn't that what every employee wants to hear? Why are you being so difficult?"

I sigh, annoyed with him, propping a hand on my hip. Well, the man doesn't seem all that ready to have me back in the company. The money has never been a problem; it's his attitude toward having me in the company that has always been a problem. And clearly, he hasn't realized that. But it is satisfying somehow to hear him wear the emotion he's dragged out of me on more than one occasion, even if its not genuine.

"I think I'm going to be alright. You can expect my resignation first thing tomorrow."

I don't wait for a reply before ending the call.

"Trouble in paradise?"

I spin around to find the most handsome man I have ever seen looking at me with a small smile. And I, not so graciously, choke on my spit.

Chapter Five

It's surprising that after all these years, I'm still able to recognize Grant at first glance. Much like how I took one look at him when we were kids and decided that I was going to be the one he went to prom with. Amongst other things.

Grant Carter stands tall in a white t-shirt and jeans, as usual. He's wearing boots and a baseball cap with a familiar logo on it, but the sun is so bright I can't make out what it is. His charming smile, the one I've seen so many times growing up, is still there. Directed either at me or at other people he'd been trying to charm.

Seeing how we dated long ago, it was safe to say I knew how that smile worked back then. It probably still does the same thing today.

Although, it doesn't excuse my lack of words or the fact that I can't even talk because I'm still fighting back the remainder of the cough that rose from the spit I unexpectedly choked on.

His skin is tanned and seems to be glowing in the warm spring sun. I force a smile on my face, and I get it for the first time—what Taylor Swift was going on about when she sang about boyish looks on men.

This man in front of me mirrors that exactly.

"Are you alright?" Grant asks taking a step forward. He extends his arm as if to pat me in comfort, and I duck out of his reach. I'd like the ground to open up and swallow me right now.

I chuckle nervously as Grant retracts his hand. The smile is still present on his face.

"Jeremy stopped me and said you were back in town and here at Josie's."

"Coffee tastes better in the morning, and they say she's the best in town," I say and conclude my sentence with a light laugh executed by only me. It's the most humiliating solo laugh I've ever performed, and I've had a lot of humiliating laughs.

Grant nods his head, as if he understands me completely. He doesn't point out that I'm wiping my hand on my pants or that I'm managing to look everywhere but at him. He's gracious in a way that I wouldn't be.

"It's nice to see you though, since no one knows how long you're going to be staying this time, and we've never managed to catch each other before."

Nodding quickly. "I'm going to be staying longer this time. I quit my job. I've moved back here and..."

Pausing and realizing, this is way too much information to unload onto someone I've only just semi-reunited with.

"Well, I better get back inside, see ya around."

Without waiting for him to reply, I turn around and hurry back into the café. Josie is grinning when I step inside.

"That was the most awkward interaction I've ever had the pleasure of witnessing through glass windows."

She doesn't get a response; I just shake my head planting it in my hands. "UGH! Why am I so awkward?" We both laugh. I then congratulate her on the café, and our conversation continues.

Later that day, making my way through town I stop at the next best shop around here.

When all my mother's friends want to get together, they do so in her bookstore with a steaming cup of coffee, supplied by Josie, and the spiciest books ever read by elderly women.

Turning my mom's copy of their current read my way and with a scrunched-up nose I said, "Oh my gosh mom!" On the cover is a young man with low-hanging jeans staring right at me in a manner that I can only describe as lusty.

"You shouldn't read things like this," I tell my mother, throwing the book on the counter. "It's not right for your heart."

My mother chuckles. "I can read whatever I want, and nothing serious is ever written in this type of book, but everyone keeps acting like it's the most scandalous thing in the world."

"It's so icky, no one ever acts that passionate mom," I state in a deadpan tone.

But honestly what would I know?

"You're just saying that because you've spent all your time reading non-fictions that aren't even memoirs. It's good you're here though, you can take care of the store while we have our little chat. Also, I heard you ran into Grant Carter today."

Oh my god, this town knows everything.

Blinking and caught without a response because, that is not the direction I thought this conversation would take. I was preparing my reply in defense of non-fictions, and now I have to talk about my awkward conversation with Grant.

"I keep forgetting that this town doesn't know how to keep a secret," I say, while throwing my mom a smile.

"It's not that. Everyone has been trying to get Grant to promise his undying love to their daughters. I've never managed to get a word in, especially since you both dated as kids. But now that you're back in town, I'm sure that I can say something to him on your behalf."

"You better be joking because I don't need you to do anything."

"When was the last time you dated someone, anyone? Maybe you should date now that you've quit your job. You always said you were too busy for it anyway. Now, you have nothing keeping you busy."

"That's not why I returned to Willow Falls. I didn't come here to meet a man."

My mother waves me off, directing me into the cashier's seat behind the desk. "Well, it won't hurt to try it out. Plus, he used to always ask about you when he first returned to Willow Falls."

"Oh, how long ago was this?"

"When he returned or when he asked about you?"

"Both?"

My mother grins like she knows something I don't. "Well, I don't think that will be of any interest to you. You should focus on resting. Forget all about Grant Carter and his interest in you. You need the rest."

How long has he been in Willow Falls?

I wanted to argue more, but my mother didn't give me the chance, picking up her book from the counter and walking out of the room, words of encouragement falling from her lips about how I really need the rest I'm seeking.

The last thing on my mind is resting, though. I start to wonder about my mother's comment about Grant's interest in me. Could that be true?

Chapter Six

I sent my resignation letter bright and early. I've had it sitting in a draft for months, and the lack of hesitation I feel when I finally hit the send button makes me chuckle.

This is a job that I had held on to for nearly all my adult life, and now, I'm tossing it into the deep end with no care in the world. And it wasn't just one boss or two that brought me to this decision. It was a decision weighing heavily on my mind for a few years now. Although the job itself and the clients I was designing for brought me happiness most days, the end result was not what I desired anymore. The environment was sucking the joy out of me.

Today, I have no plans outside of helping my mother and visiting Josie. We agreed to hang out more and catch up as much as we can. Josie has promised to give me all the updates I need to understand what is going on in the town, and I cannot wait for it.

I don't know what type of information I'm going to be regaled with, but I'm certain it won't be anything scandalous. Willow Falls isn't the type of place that can survive a scandal.

There's a soft knock on my door before it's being pushed open. My father's head appears first, and there's a small smile on his face. It's not his usual smile; it's the one he gives me when he's about to do something my mother has put him up to. His face looks guilty, but I still welcome his smile.

I take a breath and brace myself.

"Hey kiddo," he says as he's stepping into the room, leaving the door ajar, and I can tell it's a conscious effort. If I didn't know better, I'd guess that my mother is standing behind the door, paying attention to our conversation.

"Hey Dad," I say, content to play along and see where this goes. "Heading to the barn?"

My father runs the family farm but not as actively as he used to. Since his age started catching up with him, he has delegated all the heavy lifting to farmhands. Which meant he had to employ more people. However, he's still in charge of discussing supplies of farm produce and checking up on the horses, cattle, and chickens.

The discussions on which horses to lend out and which one participates in what competition are still his call to make. I like to think that it's something I can take over from him someday to help him relax a bit.

But the thing with my parents is they don't expect me to take over the family business. They can get someone to help on the farm if the work gets too much for them to handle. And so far, that's what they've been doing. But I want to at least pull my weight for the duration of my stay here.

"Yes, but my truck is currently having some issues, and I'm going to be late." He's talking without looking at me, studying the picture of both my parents resting on the nightstand. It was taken when I was seven or eight and my father is holding me on his lap as we stare at the camera.

We both look awkward in the picture, it was the first time we got our pictures professionally taken as a family. My mother had insisted on it, and my mother is the only one who looks prepared for it. Comfortable even.

"You can take my car if you want."

This gets my father's attention. He looks thrilled by the proposal, and I realize that's way too much excitement to borrow a car. I know my mother sent him in here, I just don't know why yet. But, I'll figure it out soon enough.

"I was going to ask, but I didn't know if you were going to use the car today or not. Thank you for letting me drive your fancy Audi," he says, letting out a small laugh.

I send another smile his way and wait.

It doesn't take much for the man to crack.

"Also, I was wondering, if you don't already have plans, can you take my truck to the mechanic? I'd ask your mother, but she doesn't exactly like driving that thing."

I stay quiet, sure that there is more to it. It doesn't make sense that he's this nervous about asking me to take his truck to the mechanic. The car, at some point in high school, became a joint property between me and my father. My parents bought this car and agreed it could be mine when I left for college if I took over the payments.

When Dad wasn't driving it for work, I was taking it out for ice cream runs. And if remembering correctly, the mechanic was Timothy, whose son, last I heard, became a banker, got married, and didn't bother checking up on his father.

It's the closest Willow Falls had come to a scandal. No one managed to figure out how to get in touch with the son, but it seemed like Timothy stopped caring. Gosh, he must be ancient by now though.

So who runs the garage now?

Still, keeping my cool, hoping that there's going to be more to the story and my parents are planning something more elaborate than asking me to take my father's truck to the mechanic. Maybe they want to surprise me for dinner and need me out of the house, I think to myself.

My father's eyes go wide after I stay silent for too long. "You must be really tired. Don't worry about it, I'll take the truck myself when I come back from work. I don't know what I was thinking."

"No, no," jumping to my feet. "I'll take it. I'm sorry, I thought you were joking for a second there. I thought you and Mom were trying to play a prank on me or kicking me out."

"What?" my father says again, emphasizing the *WH*. "Why would we do that?"

It makes me all the more doubtful, but before I can follow up on it, my father hands me the keys to the truck and picks up my keys from my nightstand. "We need to get it started, c'mon," he says as he's walking away. On the third try we get the truck started.

"I will see you later," he says as he shuts the door, leaving me to wonder if I've been away from home for too long or if their motive is to get me to go to the mechanic.

Adjusting my seat, I hear my car revving and look up. I noticed my mom is leaning into the window of the car, discussing something with my father. I have no idea what it is, but my mother's plans have always left me feeling uncertain.

Timothy's Garage shop sits at the edge of town, about a fifteen-minute drive. Some days, Willow Falls has its fair share of visitors, especially from tourists who need a place to stay or fix a flat. I know that Susan Granger inherited the inn from her mother, and year in and year out, the inn serves as a meeting point for a lot of artists and hobby shoppers from all over due to Willow Falls having one of the biggest summer festivals around.

I haven't been to one in a long time, but I do plan on participating in the next one.

Timothy's Garage has undergone a lot of changes since I was last here. The place looks better now, more put together. The roof has been fixed; it's no longer falling apart. The walls have been painted a dark green color that now seems to be covered in snap-on and car posters.

Clearly, Timothy got his shit together and decided to not let the garage turn into a pile of garbage. Or maybe his son came back and took over the place?

Business seems to be booming if the number of cars in the garage is anything to go by. I don't know much about cars, but the one sitting in front of me is black and sleek, and I've seen a lot of them in the city, but here in Willow Falls, it seems out of place. Cars like this don't belong in quaint country towns.

A head rolls out from under the car, and I can't help the scream that escapes me. Stumbling backward and noticing it's Grant, he's hurrying out with his arms open to catch me before I fall.

I clutch my chest, willing my breathing to calm down. Why didn't I hear all his tinkering at first? Now that he's standing there and the frantic pounding of my heart is slowing down, the quiet settles in.

"What are you doing here?" I ask, looking him up and down as if he's some anomaly in the garage.

"I work here?" he replies.

"What do you mean you work here? Where's Timothy?" I ask, looking past him to get a closer look at the interiors of the garage, hoping that Timothy is going to swagger out in that manly way of his and tell Grant off.

"He's not available. He's off somewhere, enjoying his retirement."

"Oh, my mother didn't mention that to me."

Of course she didn't.

I realized why my father was in my room earlier. This is my mother's elaborate plan.

If I had any idea the shop changed ownership, I wouldn't have waltzed in here so casually. I was expecting the older gentleman, Timothy. But instead, I got Grant Carter. Shirtless. Oh my word, the things going through my head right now.

He has abs for days.

Those sharp ridges, and each section carefully defined. There are eight of them in total, and I've heard that eight packs are fairly hard to come by, which means that he put in the work to look like a Calvin Klein model. He's like a walking, talking thirst trap.

I now understand why the women in the comment section of these videos are so feral. His sex appeal radiates off him, and I can't look away. It's just glaring at me, and I have no choice but to keep looking. This is marvelous.

I let my eyes trail all over his body, the curve of his neck, his soft skin, the black stains of a day's job on his jeans, to his lips and his eyes that are looking right at me with raised brows. Oh my gosh, my hands are on his bare arms.

Is it hot out here?

Again, I choke and come back to my senses a lot quicker than expected.

"You're staring," Grant says, and I don't dare to ask what he means. I don't even look at him. I can feel my cheeks blush and I wipe my palms on my pants. I tug on my hair even though I have it wrapped up in a ponytail, thinking I was going to help on the farm today.

"I brought my father's truck," I say, throwing my thumb behind me, in the direction of the truck. I still don't dare to look at him, scared that he'll be able to pick up my mortification from just a single look in my eyes.

"You can look all you want," Grant says as he passes by me. "I don't mind."

His voice is deep and smooth.

Goosebumps.

Rooted to this spot just long enough to gain composure and act normal, I then walk back to the truck where Grant is already looking at it.

"What seems to be the problem?"

Shrugging my shoulders. "I have no idea. Possibly an oil change. It takes a while to start. Dad didn't mention it to me, and I was under the impression that he had already discussed it with you. How did you manage to be here? How did you convince Timothy to leave?"

Grant hums as he throws open the hood of the truck. "I promised him I'd take care of the place."

"How long have you been in Willow Falls?"

"Longer than you, clearly. Did you really quit your job?"

"I needed a change of scenery. City life was starting to bore me, and Willow Falls seems like a good place to set my foot down until I figure things out."

Grant nods his head. "So, you're not going to be here for a long time then? When the weather is fine for you, you'll head out? I don't blame you, Willow Falls has those healing properties. I also came here to rest my head, and I've decided to make a life here."

"I don't remember you being here the last time I was here."

"You haven't been here for a long time. I was here a year after the last year you showed up. Nine years for me."

I nod my head, knowing the Christmas I was last here, 6 years ago, I was only here for that day.

"You seem to be doing fine. I guess the city was nice to you."

I chuckle lightly. "I can't complain, I guess."

We both remain quiet, and I hope my words are believable. I have a mountain of things I can complain about. For instance, Greg Jr. refuses to accept my resignation letter and demands to speak to me. He keeps insisting that we can work through whatever demands I might have. Completely disregarding my demand to be left alone. The noises in the city are just irritating in themselves. I have no friends and no hobbies out there.

"I'll check the engine," Grant says.

"I'll come back for the truck," I throw over my shoulder as I turn around to walk away from the garage. Seeing Grant shirtless is one thing, but I have no idea what will become of me and my thoughts if I have to see him actually work without a shirt on.

"Alexis, how are you getting home?"

Shoot.

"Um, do you think you can drop me off? "

Chapter Seven

"You did what?" Josie says, getting between me and the eggs she's counting. "Tell me you're joking. I can't believe you actually went to Grant's garage and he gave you a ride."

"Grant's garage? What.... He owns the place?"

"Not quite. But he works there most of the time. Other times, however, he works over here."

I place the eggs we gathered in the basket Josie showed up with. Sent by her mother to buy eggs and milk for their next batch of baked goods, Josie looks too pleased with herself for bearing witness to all of this drama.

I freeze.

"Where exactly do you mean here?"

Josie looks around before waving her hand around the farm. "He's the farmhand. Didn't your parents mention it? It's really interesting that they needed you to take the truck to him when he could have just fixed it here."

He's what?!

Blinking once and then again, looking at Josie and hoping that she's joking about Grant working on the farm. I know that someone comes around to handle a lot of the work and farm duties, but I've never met the person. They usually show up later in the night or super early in the morning, and I always pretend to be asleep during these times.

"You're joking. Please be joking." It's then I realize, "Oh my gosh his hat. It had the farm logo on it."

"What are we joking about?" my mother asks, coming into the kitchen with a basket tucked under her arm.

"Grant works here?"

My mother stops short, sparing Josie a look, which causes her to duck her head as if she's just been reprimanded.

"He lends a hand here and there," Mom says as nonchalantly as she can pretend to. "Did I not mention it?"

"You didn't," I say, my tone accusatory.

I cannot believe my mother would keep something like this from me.

"You know I'd remember if you did. Why didn't you just tell me he worked here instead of getting Dad to ask me to drop off his truck? I must have looked like an idiot."

"I hope you managed to talk to him this time. I'm really trying to set you up with the town's most eligible bachelor, and it works well in our favor that he works here too."

I gave her my worst scowl. Which really doesn't even qualify as a scowl.

" I just wanted you to meet him outside of this space. Now, what did you two talk about?"

"That's not important," I say at the same time Josie says, "Nothing, she choked on her spit again."

"Do you not know how to talk to men?" my mother asks with a frown on her face. "When I was your age, I was a champion at catching all the boys' attention. You're still too young to waste away. I'm sure that you can convince him to look your way. Remember when you were in love?"

"We were never in love."

Were we?

"Oh my god," Josie says and claps her hand. "I completely forgot about that. You went to prom together and would not leave each other's sides! You two were so cute. Girl, you were so in love."

Then, as if it's the funniest thing she's ever heard, Josie breaks into a laugh. "This is perfect. It can be like a reunion. A small-town romance. Trust me, Alexis, this will be good for you."

"You should go," I say, gathering Josie's things into the woven basket she came with. "You've said enough, and you shouldn't be encouraging my mother's delusion."

"Delusions?" my mother says, clearly affronted.

I don't take the bait, handing Josie her basket with a firm look on my face.

"You should tell me how it goes with Grant. He's a hard one to catch," Josie retorts. "A lot of ladies have been trying to get with him, and he's a hit with the tourists when they come to town. It's a good thing your parents took the initiative to safeguard him for you."

I all but shove Josie out of the house, telling her I'll see her tomorrow as she gives the barn cat a scratch on the head and waves bye.

"Why didn't you tell me Grant works here?"

"You haven't been here for a long time. And it's not like you have anything to worry about, right?"

I know my mother enough to not reward her with a response.

That night, I keep tossing and turning, listening for the sign of someone showing up to the house. Someone other than my parents. I know I should go to bed, but I'm just unable to sleep.

Over and over, I tell myself to just go to sleep. There is no reason for me to keep worrying about Grant. Sure, we have some history, but that's all in the past. Nothing for me to worry about now. Is there?

Still, every creak in the gate has me lying here waiting, listening for the voices. I could go downstairs and play it off, say I'm unable to sleep because I'm worrying about work and what I'm going to do with my life.

Greg Jr. hasn't left me alone since I sent in my resignation letter. He's been calling me so much it's starting to bother me. If he doesn't stop, I plan on reaching out to the HR department and complaining.

Grant, on the other hand, is not someone I can call a department to take care of. If he was working at just Timothy's Garage, I wouldn't have to run into him all the time. Maybe when I go into town or if we end up in the same space, but if he works on our family's farm, I would have to see him all the time.

Farmhands are essential to a farm's growth, but the thing about farmhands is they're easily integrated into the family. It doesn't take long for the family they're working for to start treating them like they're a son or daughter.

And with my father being unable to move around the farm like he usually does, Grant's position is very important and vital to keep things running. My mother is much too old to do the heavy lifting, and I don't know how the farm operates outside of what I was already used to as a child and teenager.

"Grant," I hear my mother's voice ring through the house, the thrill in her voice unmistakable. "How are you?"

Grant must reply, but his voice is low, which means my mother is going over and beyond to let me know that Grant has made his presence known.

I lie on the bed, but my resolve cracks by the third minute. I get to my feet and check myself in the full-length mirror in the corner of the room. I look around the pale green walls of the room, my childhood pictures still hanging, and I make a mental note to take it all down and possibly repaint the room to something more grown-up.

My mind immediately conjures up the off-white color of my previous apartment, but I shake my head and shudder at the idea of having to revert back to the life I just freed myself from.

Maybe I should just paint this room like a rainbow.

"There you are," my mother says the second I reach the bottom of the stairs. "I was starting to worry that you fell asleep up there."

"Working on your resume to send off to the big corporations?" Grant asks with a smile on his face, and I hold back a groan as I force a smile on my face.

"Wait," my mother says and points to Grant, "she told you she quit her job?"

"I didn't tell him anything," I'm quick to state. "He just happened to be there when I had to speak to my boss. I mean ex-boss. Not the point. He was just in the vicinity when I took the call, and he was eavesdropping."

"It was a public space," Grant says, complete with an eye roll. "And I haven't seen you in forever, so I thought hello was in order, but apparently, I was the only one who thought we were on hello terms."

"Alexis," my mother scolds before I can get the chance to defend myself. "He's really stretching himself thin between working for us and the garage. He practically owns the garage now, you know, but that's beside the point. You should be a lot nicer to him, especially since you'll be working closely with him."

"I'll be what?"

"Working closely with him. Since you're already here, you should help out as much as you can. Don't you think so?"

I raise my brow at my mother, wondering where she's going with this. This is the woman who told me to take my time adjusting in Willow Falls. What is it she said when I had complained about not knowing where my place was in all of this?

There was no need to figure everything out right now. My parents never seemed to expect a future on the farm for me, so the pressure to step into that role never felt real. But suddenly, working closely with Grant is the expectation.

"Grant knows everything," my mother continues, ignoring the look I'm sending her way. "And I trust you're a fast learner. All those top scores in school should be evidence of that."

I pause, giving my mother the chance to think about the words that are falling out of her mouth. If I've ever been described as stubborn, then it's a trait I had to have gotten from someone.

My father is the most easy-going man on the planet, and this is evidenced by the fact that he's sitting in his favorite seat watching this drama unfold like it's a programmed show with a giant smile on his face.

My mother maintains eye contact as if waiting for me to say something, but any argument I have ready dies from my mother's firm stare.

Returning to Willow Falls is supposed to be relaxing and healing. I didn't account for meeting my ex here or my mother's determination to play cupid.

Chapter Eight

Instead of my alarm clock, my mother wakes me up early. Since I no longer startle awake in the early hours of the morning from fear of missing a deadline, I actually get a full night's rest. I'm thankful for that.

"You'll be working with Grant," my mother says like we didn't already have the discussion last night. "Grant shows up really early. It's why you've never bumped into him here, but since we already have an agreement, you should head out to seize the day and all that. Isn't that how busy city folks say it?"

Instead of replying, I focus on getting ready quickly, which is the only reason why I show up earlier than Grant to the barn.

"I've been doing these chores for years now, I could probably do them blindfolded or in my sleep. Let's just start small," Grant tells me. It's too early for me to be up, but I'm used to this. This is like my life in the city, except the nerves here are from wondering if Grant usually looks this handsome or if he's making an effort because of me. I'm delusional for thinking that, though.

He looks so put together—wearing overalls of his own, dark blue where mine are dark green, and a cowboy hat even though the sun is not out yet. One would think he's about to model for Wrangler or become the next "Farmer Wants a Wife".

"What is it that you do then?"

"Nothing a city worker like you can't handle," Grant says, and I roll my eyes. I'm starting to get tired of him mentioning the city like he didn't work there a long time ago. If I'm being precise about the timing, it hasn't been that long.

"I'm sure you know I used to do all of this as a kid before I went off to college and then work. There's nothing you're doing that I haven't done before. So maybe don't bring up my job in the city, and I won't try to show you up."

Grant smirks and tilts his head to the side as if I'm amusing him. "We don't just milk cows around here or fit saddles, Alexis. It's more than that now."

"And I'll know all about it if you actually start showing me what it is about rather than just talking about it."

He smiles again and heads out of the barn. "I'll start by bringing you up to speed with what the farm has to offer nowadays. Eggs you already know, but we have a few livestock we rear for butchering."

He looks at me as if the city was supposed to sell on the idea of being repulsed by the death of animals. This is where I grew up, and if I don't know that much about the farm, then I have no business trying to help around.

"We also have a few new horses; I'm sure you know where the stables are. Your father has been kind enough to let me know that your favorite horse passed a few years ago and you haven't been to the stables since then. So, we don't have to go out during our time together."

"I'm not traumatized or anything," I say, voice tight from the insinuation. "I just haven't been around enough to be at the stables to see them."

Grant stops walking abruptly, making me bump into him.

"Don't just stop like that, give a girl a warning," I tell him as I create space between us.

"You're so defensive around me, and I don't like that," Grant grinds out. "I don't know how I'm coming off when I speak to you, but I want you to know that I'm not trying to accuse you of anything. I don't expect you to know all about the farm. You haven't been here in ten years, and that's a decade worth of changes you weren't available for. I've been here for nine years, and I've been working on this farm each of those nine years because your family needed the help and I wasn't doing anything else."

"I'm not being defensive," I bite back, and this time, I'm aware of how defensive my tone sounds.

"Okay." Grant nods his head, but he clearly doesn't believe me because he can hear the same tone in my voice. "We'll just work on that then."

I don't bother replying because I know that whatever I say will take on the same tone.

"Early mornings are just us cleaning out the barn and stalls, then feeding," he goes on to tell me as he resumes walking, giving me a breakdown of how things are done.

There are a total of six workers on the farm, and each of them help in whatever way they can. As the head of the farmhands, Grant is responsible for sharing the duties between them. He has the right to switch out routines and hire or fire anyone as necessary. But he still makes sure to get my father's input, and so far, he hasn't had to fire anyone.

Something he's grateful for because losing a job isn't easy to get through. And as if we're the best of friends, and it's any other conversation, he tells me, "I got fired from my last job."

I have no previous experience talking about job loss with anyone, so I don't know what to say in response to that. It was once recommended that I take an empathy class by Greg Jr. because I didn't give the right type of reply to his troubles.

There were a lot of things in Greg Jr.'s life that I suffered through hearing about, and admittedly, I didn't always know how to react to it because no one I knew had those types of problems.

"Oh," is what I settle on saying because there are no other words that come into my mind.

Grant just nods. "I don't think I could fire anyone and have them wonder why they weren't the ones that were chosen to stay. Even if you explain it to them, you need to convince yourself that you're making the right decision. The man who told me they were laying me off couldn't even meet my eyes. I felt bad for him."

The only words that make their way out of my mouth are, "Oh. Um, yeah."

"You've always had a way with words."

I can't help the laugh that slips out. It's loud and in my head, I can still hear Grant tell me there's no need for me to be so defensive around him. It's freeing, this little life I could live in Willow Falls.

Standing there in thought, I happen to glance out the barn window to see the sky changing from gray to orange as the morning sun begins to shine.

Chapter Nine

"One year."

"You can't be serious."

"We'll let you have a one-year paid vacation. Don't even bother coming back for this project; we'll present it ourselves and compensate you accordingly. Hell, we'll call it a sabbatical."

I'm too stunned by the offer. I know I'm a good architect, but this is too much even for me. A one-year paid vacation is not an offer anyone I know has ever received. It's not even a valuable offer. Who pays you for one year to do nothing?

Greg Jr. has had a lot of employees quit on him; I wasn't his first. And one time, he managed to get one of them to come back with so many offers only to fire him within a week.

It's hilarious that Greg Jr. is trying the same tactic with me, knowing full well that I know all of this. How does he expect me to show up to work, knowing that I'm going to get the boot?

"Are you serious?" I ask, my voice carrying disbelief.

"It's the deal of a lifetime, and I'm offering it to you. We value you in this company, and we want you to know that."

"Greg," I say, since calling him sir hasn't gotten me anywhere. "I don't want to come back and work for you. The years I worked for you were the most miserable of my existence. Why you think I would come back for a repeat performance really baffles me. It isn't about the money; it's about how you keep taking things from me. How you keep letting me have things that I already deserve while making it look like you're doing me a favor. I have no idea why you think I would walk my ass right back into that hellhole just to live through that misery again. Because of what? The money you're throwing my way, no, I don't need it. If you call me again, I'll have to start thinking about filing a harassment claim."

I don't wait for a reply before hanging up. Thinking to myself, I should have never even picked up the phone.

A deep breath steadies my nerves. Quitting hadn't come with the expectation that Greg Jr. would be this persistent to keep me. If that much value had truly existed to the team, real effort would have been made to grant vacation days before the walkout. He wouldn't have made me meet deadlines that were so unreasonable.

He would have respected me as his employee.

My plan was to work with them for a couple of years, rise in the ranks, make meaningful connections, and then open my own company. But my growth rate had been so slow that it destroyed my confidence. I used to be the best in my class. I gave up a lot of things for that company, and all that did was destroy my ambition. And somehow, they expected me to come back now that I was ready to move on for the sake of my own sanity.

I don't need it anymore. They're a little too late for it now.

I step out of the house; my mother has gone off for her book club meeting. They are meeting somewhere else, while my father, having had his truck returned the previous day, has taken to driving himself to meet a couple of friends for drinks.

Having Grant in charge really does put my father at rest.

I make my way down to the stables. Since my little talk with Grant, I haven't been able to get it out of my head. It wasn't a result of trauma, but when Daisy, my favorite horse, died, I didn't have any reason to keep making the trip down to the stables. I held such a special connection with her, and I was crushed after she passed.

Unlike most of the structures on the farm, the stables are further from the main house and other barn.

My parents didn't want the horses near the cattle or chickens. Whatever disease any animal got, they tried to contain it within those animals.

And if it did spread to the horses, it was a pain. They are, after all, the money makers of the farm.

Our horses are the finest racehorses in the whole of Willow Falls and its surroundings. When Daisy was alive, she used to be the most awarded racehorse.

Whatever horse my father decided on was considered the best in the breed, and in their line of business, that's not something people take lightly.

The horses are the main attraction of the farm. The other livestock are just a means of filling the empty spaces and bringing in more income. They also help to provide for the businesses in town.

The stable is a large space that has been separated into sections. In total, there are ten sections. Each of them contains one horse for each section. The younger horses are kept in a separate stable to not overwhelm them with the older ones once they're of age. I approach one of the horses and stretch out my hand. The horse takes a tentative step towards me, sniffs my hand, and takes a step backward. The thing about horses is you have to get them to trust you before they'll let you touch them.

I'm a patient woman, and more than that, I know my way to a horse's heart. Bribery seems to be the way to go. I dip my hand into the pockets of my pants and pull out the sugar cubes I stuffed in there.

The horse neighs and takes a step forward, sniffing my hand and eating the sugar cube. I grin with satisfaction and pet her, feeding her the sugar at intervals. Looking at the tag by the door, I read her name, Aster. Amusement with my father's choice to stick with wildflower names has my mouth turning up in a small smile.

"Fancy seeing you here."

The voice startles me, and I whip my head around. My movement startles Aster, and she neighs and steps back.

Grant enters the stables like an apparition. He's holding a metal bucket, and the last rays of the evening sun pour into the barn, lighting him up in an ethereal fashion. The way his overalls hug his thighs, he's a walking daydream.

I feel spit pool in my mouth, but this time, I'm determined to not let a repeat of what happened all the times I've met with Grant occur. I swallow as I watch him dump feed into the bins for the horses, patting each one as he goes.

"I told you I wasn't traumatized by the death of Daisy."

"I didn't accuse you of being traumatized. I only mentioned it once, and you got defensive about it."

I step out of the way to let him feed Aster. "You didn't go to the garage today?"

It's an attempt to divert the conversation from myself.

"I'm not the only worker the garage has just like I'm not the only farmhand on this farm. Both the garage and the farm will function properly without me."

"My father doesn't think the farm will make it without you."

Grant chuckles. "Your father likes to talk me up. It's a pleasure to know he keeps the habit up in front of you."

I shrug my shoulders, unsure of what to say after that. If I'm being honest, I'm curious about Grant. More specifically, I'm concerned about why he returned to Willow Falls. No one here seems to know the reason why he returned home so suddenly.

But my mother tells me it was much like my return, except that Grant's had come with the rain. His parents also don't know, but they're not forcing him to tell them either. They accepted that the city just didn't work out for him but were saddened by the distance his leaving had created between them.

Getting fired from his job was what he told me, but I want to know why he didn't just apply for another job out there. He's an excellent worker, honestly. Anybody would be lucky to have him on their team. My father is over the moon about him helping on the farm.

UGH, here's the pot calling the kettle black.

Lost in a daydream, curiosity drifts toward which city he had been in.

Grant breaks my thoughts. "You're staring."

"I'm not."

"It's an observation, not an accusation."

"I don't feel accused."

"Then don't get defensive. You weren't always like this."

"You would know," I say.

Grant chuckles like it's a weak comeback. "I should, and I do know. I mean, I dated you."

You see, I 've thought about it a million times, the topic of us dating coming up, but I never imagined it would be like this.

"That was a long time ago, and I've changed. For the better."

Grant chuckles again and turns his attention to me. "I'm still not accusing you of anything. And anyways, I thought you were great back then. Still are."

I open my mouth to say something, but I don't know what I can say that won't come off as defensive. I watch as Grant walks up to me, each step calculated as if he's giving me a chance to walk away.

The thing with me is I don't back away from a dare—or any insinuation of it. That's why I stand straight and wait for the man to come to me. He stops in front of me, and I feel all the air float out of my lungs.

My breath hitches, and I watch him, maintaining eye contact and ignoring the way my heart is hammering in my chest. All of the questions I had for him escaped my mind, and the only thing I can think about is how manly he smells. The fresh scent of his body wash mixed with his sweat. It's like a mixture of cedar and cinnamon, sweet, salty, and desirable.

I want to lean in and press my body to his for no reason other than to see how he'd react. His eyes twinkle in amusement as if he can read my mind.

Picking a piece of straw out of my hair, he leans down and whispers, "I don't know if anyone has said this to you, but *I'm really glad you're back, Alexis.*" Then he stands up straight and asks, "Have you made it to the field yet?"

I don't respond. I just exhale.

What just happened?

Chapter Ten

I wake up with my stomach in knots, but this time, it's for a different reason. Grant's last words rang in my head, rocking me to sleep and then forcing me out of the little sleep I did manage to grab.

He's glad that I'm back in town. Grant is glad that I'm back in town. I would like to know what that meant exactly and wonder if I should visit the wildflower fields. Did they change? What did he mean by that...

With a sigh, I get out of bed, telling myself to let it be. When I see Josie later in the day, I'll get around to dissecting Grant's words and what my excitement about those words mean.

I get ready for the day. Again, I'll have to shadow Grant, but I have no idea what today's job will entail. My mother was supposed to let me know what our schedule will look like, but I rushed out of the stable last night and up to my room, promising my mother we would speak tomorrow.

That's today.

I head downstairs to find my mother already there sipping on a cup of coffee. My father is seated next to her, and they're both looking up at me as I make my way down the stairs.

The air smells of fried eggs and coffee, and I take in another whiff, hoping to catch the scent of bacon.

YES!

"Morning, sweetheart," my father greets me as I place a kiss on his cheek. "How was your night? You turned in really early."

My mother says nothing, maintaining eye contact as she keeps sipping on her cup of coffee. I try to not look towards her because I know she knows. It's my mom. If anything, she is the reason Grant showed up to the stables.

That woman is an expert at putting one and two together.

"I was exhausted from working in the barn all day. I wanted to rest up for today because I had the impression that today would be tough."

I shrug my shoulders and walk further into the kitchen, placing a kiss on my mother's cheek, who tilts her head to the side to accept it. I pour myself a cup of coffee and take a seat next to my mother at the round table. I steal a piece of bacon from my mother's plate and smile sheepishly when she sends a glare my way.

"You were tossing a lot in your room," my mother says offhandedly, placing the cup of coffee on the table before reaching for her notebook. "I kept hearing the rustling of sheets."

"The walls are not that thin," I say immediately, looking from my mother to my father. My father shakes his head with a crestfallen look on his face, which lets me know that I have just given myself away in a situation that was perfectly orchestrated by my mother.

"So, you were tossing and turning then," my mother says, putting on her glasses, but the smirk on her face is obvious. "Any reason why?"

"Nope," I say and take a sip of my coffee. "I'm just still getting used to all of this."

My mother nods her head vigorously. "Well, we have a busy day ahead of us. Your father still has the discussion meeting about the horses to attend, and I have to see to the delivery of some of the farm produce. I'm taking Silas with me, which means you are going to work alongside Grant."

I already know this, so I nod my head in understanding. "What exactly are we going to be doing?"

"That will be up to Grant. He should be somewhere on the farm, I saw him a little earlier. Try not to scare him off with the awkwardness hovering over you whenever you see him."

"There's no awkwardness," I scoff, but my mother is already getting to her feet. "He's going to need coffee and maybe make more bacon. Try to make sure you fix sandwiches for lunch, I'll be back a little late."

"Oh, ok. Thanks, Mom." This is going to be easy for me to see through.

The task for today:

1. Give coffee to Grant

2. Work with him for however long it takes to get the job done.

3. Make a sandwich for both of us.

4. Go and see Josie to unpack all of what happened last night.

I shake my head as my father places a kiss on my cheek and waves goodbye, squeezing his cowboy hat in his hands. I watch him go with a smile on my face. Someday, I'll be the one going to these meetings so getting my head together is really important.

Thinking about Grant and deciphering what his words meant, looking for something that isn't there isn't going to do me any good. Grant's here to help on the farm and also guide me into knowing what I need to know about taking over for my father.

Is that what I really want, though?

That question has been lurking in my mind for a while, and I've been putting off thinking about it anymore. Coming back to Willow Falls has been the plan, but when I originally had the idea, it was for the sake of relaxing, finding myself, reconnecting with a town I was certain would heal me. I eventually would return to the city. Right?

In a way, I had hoped that I'd feel more like myself for a while before heading back to the city and doing the job that will fill me with more value and for a company that will appreciate all my efforts. Now, I'm wondering if what I truly need is right here.

From the kitchen window, I catch sight of a figure moving, and that pulls me out of my head. It's Grant, and he's coming towards the house. He moves with the type of purpose I never caught in any of the city men.

One foot in front of another.

The plaid shirt he's wearing atop the white tee clings to him, drawing focus on his muscles. I wonder how many times he goes to the gym to be able to achieve such a glorious physique.

I sigh and lean into the hand my cheek is resting on. It puts a frown on my face and I sit up, looking down at the offending hand because how did it even come up to the table, and when did my cheek rest on it? And to stare at Grant, no less.

It's true that he looks amazing; I won't lie, but it isn't enough reason to lose my mind over it.

When he comes up to the backdoor, I sit up and fix my dress because it's what a normal person should do when they're about to see someone so early in the day.

Two rapid knocks and the door is being pushed open, giving me no time to figure out what to do with my hands, so I pick up my cup of coffee rapidly and spill a little as Grant steps through the door.

He takes his hat off when he sees me and wears the most brilliant smile I have ever seen on a man. It's not fair that the universe is ignoring all my efforts and presenting Grant in a manner that makes me blush profusely.

"Morning, Wildflower," Grant says, and it startles me because it's been a while since anybody called me that. In fact, no one except Grant called me that, and since I left Willow Falls, I never met anyone who managed to pick up the habit.

"Wildflower?"

"Is that okay? Does no one call you that anymore?"

Instant butterflies.

It was an odd thing to mention. Especially when it was Grant who came up with that name and no one else used it.

"Coffee?" I say instead and pour him a cup without getting a response. Grant looks amused by my reaction. He picks up the cup I poured him and takes a sip while maintaining eye contact.

"You've been doing that a lot lately," he teases.

Was I staring.... again?

I look away, clearing my throat. "So, what's the task for today?"

Grant pulls the mug away from his face. "You're going to love it."

⚘

It's been nearly an hour, and I can say that I don't love it.

The barn smells terrible, more than anything I've ever experienced. Although, I will be the first person to tell you how great horses are, how amazingly and gracefully they exist. Horses have always been the main attraction here, but I've never once thought I would be subjected to cleaning their stables. It has been so long since I've been exposed to this; it will take some getting used to again.

From the corner of my eyes, I can see Grant focusing. Although it feels like he's waiting for me to break down and complain first. I'm determined to not give him the satisfaction. I'm going to keep going until we are done, and then I'm going to take a long bath and put this day behind me. Thankfully I spilled my coffee on my dress and ended up putting pants on.

All the horses are out running in the fields grazing, and Grant has given me the chance to clean Aster's stable since I've been so drawn to her. I had wanted to argue, but Grant picked that moment to take off the plaid shirt, in what seemed like slow motion.

I feel like Ray J is going to start playing *"Sexy Can I"*.

It was a bad moment for me to realize that the t-shirt wasn't a t-shirt at all; it was a cutoff. A cutoff that put his arms on display. Josie will be happy to know that I did not choke on my own spit again. A feat that isn't easy to achieve given all the adversities that are being thrown my way.

After taking both shirts off like working shirtless is normal for him, Grant had started shoveling dirt into a wheelbarrow. I needed some time to regain my composure.

That was an hour or so ago.

Now I'm shoveling the last pile out of Aster's stable when I notice Grant standing next to me, sipping water from a glass cup. He's watching me work with a smile on his face, and I know him enough to know that he's about to say something that will have me shaking my head.

"What is it?"

"You should finish that up. We still have more to do."

"More? What more could we possibly have to do?" As I get my last question out, he starts walking away.

I'm drenched in sweat, and I don't even want to think about the smell. This is the hardest I've ever worked in my life. I make my way to the fields and decide to sit underneath the large oak tree, next to the space the horses are allowed to run around in.

If anything, I experience a sense of relief and achievement. I close my eyes and take in a deep breath, taking note of the way my chest swells with it. The birds sing in the air, and I can hear the hooves of the horses hit the ground as they run around. I breathe in the scent of the wildflowers.

They're my favorite.

"You did better than I expected," Grant says and takes a seat next to me. Something cold touches my forehead, and my eyes fly open to find a glass of water hovering over my face.

"Sit up," Grant says. "You worked really hard. I thought you'd give up after cleaning your second stable, but you persisted. It was really impressive."

I let myself soak up the compliment. When was the last time I received a compliment like this? I grab the glass of water from him and take a sip, noticing he put his shirt back on and thinking of what to say next.

I decide on rolling my eyes and following it up with, "Just because I lived in the city doesn't mean I forgot what it means to work on the farm."

But did living in the city cause me to forget this life?

Grant laughs. "You grew up with a lot of farmhands. What are you talking about?"

"I helped out a lot. I knew a fair share of what was going on around here."

Grant nods his head. "I believe you."

Does he believe me? There's the way Grant keeps looking at me like he has so much to say, but I have no intention of giving him the nudge he needs to bring it up.

Of course, Grant doesn't need me to give him a nudge, he goes for it all by himself. "I still haven't gotten over the fact that you're really here, Lex. Hell, I didn't think I'd ever see you again. You didn't come back home, and I was starting to lose hope."

Grant's words and the use of the nickname make me laugh nervously. "What, were you waiting for me?"

Grant laughs too, except there is nothing nervous about his tone. "I mean, with the way you left town, and you called once to say you couldn't go on with our relationship. You stopped taking my calls."

"*You* didn't call."

"I called a lot, too much; you said it was starting to bother you. You promised to call back when you figured things out, and that never happened."

I open my mouth to argue, but the words never make it out. I remember it differently, but now that I'm hearing it from Grant with the vulnerability in his words, I can tell that I'm the one at fault.

A promise had been made to call once things were figured out, but that call was never made.

"It was too much," I said finally. "It's not an excuse, but I was sort of lost and being one of the few from Willow Falls who actually left meant something to me. I wanted to focus on being more. I wanted to have so much, and it felt like Willow Falls was holding me back, so I wanted to cut it all off. I'm so sorry, Grant. I just always thought leaving here meant becoming something big."

"I was holding you back?"

"That's not what I'm saying," I whisper. I open my mouth to refute more, but nothing comes out. I look at Grant and find him looking at me with a frown on his face. "It was really hard, and I didn't know how to explain it to you. College was tough, and I was scared."

"It wasn't a walk in the park for me either," Grant says and gets to his feet. "I wish you didn't make the decision for the both of us. I would have still loved to try. I wanted to try."

His words cut right through me, but I don't move to stop him when he gets up to leave. What could I say that would be a justification for the way I treated him?

Chapter Eleven

S leep has been something I've always struggled with, but this time it isn't work that keeps me up all night. I'm tossing and turning because the man I dated long ago implied that I was wrong for throwing him to the curb.

Maybe throwing him to the curb is the absolute wrong way to refer to this, but my head is on fire. Every time I close my eyes to force sleep my way, Grant's face keeps popping up, looking at me like I broke his heart.

It also broke mine.

I take a deep breath to calm myself. This is something that I can solve by counting sheep if only the said sheep will stay put and stop running around. I shoot up from the bed and let out a muffled scream into my pillow. I don't want my parents rushing into the room like something bad happened without knowing that their farmhand is solely responsible for driving me to the brink of craziness.

I get up from the bed and start to pace the room.

This is all Grant's fault. Willow Falls is supposed to heal me, not add more to my stress. Nights are supposed to be for sleeping and reflecting about the niceties of the day passed, but Grant had to hit me with the past.

"Of course, college was going to be tough for him too," I whisper to myself furiously. "It has always been a hard place to cope. But why isn't he grateful that I decided to give him the space he'd need to figure things out? Wasn't that the right thing to do?"

When I broke up with Grant, it had been the right thing at the time. I didn't want to feel like I was holding him back from something. I didn't have the time to do anything other than feel miserable and bury myself in my schoolwork, so I thought Grant would be doing the same, or at the very least, he would have the time to meet other people.

The only other alternative was to keep texting each other, calling when we were too tired to even talk, falling asleep with the call still on, forcing the belief that it was romantic when it really wasn't, and we were wasting good money on phone bills. We didn't have the time to meet up and have the romance we once felt.

I did us both a favor; why was Grant acting like he didn't know that?

Why am I thinking about him so much?

I drop back on the bed and run my hand through my hair. Why can't I shut my brain off and worry about this tomorrow? It's all the energy still running through me from the day. I just need a way to exhaust myself, and at this time the only thing I can do is clean out my room.

There are a lot of trinkets from my childhood that I should get rid of. Clothes that I'm no longer wearing, objects that I've been pretending have sentimental value. All of that needs to go so I can put up things I actually need and use. My skincare products do need somewhere to go.

With another sigh, I get to work, filling trash bags with items I no longer need. I should sort them out, but the point of the entire exercise is to not do a good job; it's to do a job that gets me too tired to move. A job that will send me right to sleep.

I don't know how long I've been at this cleaning exercise, but I'm working on the closet when I stumble upon it.

It's a small metal box that used to contain chocolates, the very one Grant had shown up with on our very first date. I remember that I blushed a lot, especially since I wasn't expecting it. It took me a while to finish the chocolates, mostly because I tried to preserve them for as long as I could.

Josie tried to take one, and I remember being strongly against sharing them. I took one and split it in so many different ways as opposed to shoving the individual pieces in my mouth at once.

I settle on the floor to get a better look at the items in the box. I know for certain that the ticket from our first date is also in here. Opening the can, the first thing I'm greeted with is the dried flower from the corsage Grant gave me at prom.

It was a wildflower, and its freshness is preserved by the tape it's stuck between. Josie had told me I was too sentimental after saying she had no idea what happened to her own corsage.

But I really liked Grant, and it made sense that I would try to keep all the memories. Maybe our relationship was more romantic than I thought.

There's also a written note from him. There used to be a collection because Grant loved to leave me notes throughout the day, wishing me a good morning, afternoon, lunch break. Honestly, he'd leave me little notes whenever he could.

The smile on my face widens as I read his note:

Hey Wildflower,

Hope your day is going great. I miss you. Xoxo.

I let out a shaky breath as I read the nickname. I forgot that Grant had asked me out in the wildflower field just behind the barn because he said it reminded him so much of me. It was our favorite spot.

It's not something I've given a lot of thought to, but now, faced with memories of a past I desperately tried to escape, I wonder what my life would have been like if I didn't cut things off with everyone.

I remember the email Grant sent me. I read it over again and again, wondering what to say or if I should say anything at all. Then days blurred into each other, his texts stopped coming, the calls started to fade, and then there was silence.

I wouldn't admit it, but the days after the silence were the hardest to accept because it meant that Grant had understood what I wanted. At least that's what I thought I wanted. Hell, I didn't know if he even truly understood my reasons, but it was clear that he accepted it. That he was going to respect it.

It made me want to die a little. Instead of calling and telling him that I was sorry for cutting him off, for treating him the way I did, I went in the opposite direction.

I picked up my books and gave that all my attention; that's my reason for ending things. I put my school and then my job before everyone else.

Meeting Grant the next day is not as awkward as I imagined. I have no way of telling if it's because we have history between us or if it's Grant's unwillingness to let things be awkward.

Whatever it is, I'm grateful that I don't have to work in a tense environment.

"What's the task for today?" I ask as we walk down the field. The sun is mild on our skin, but I know that in no time, it will be beating down on us. That's why my straw hat is hanging behind me.

Grant is dressed in a loose hanging green shirt and loose fitting jeans. He's wearing boots, and it's hard for me to imagine what our task will be today if we're not in the barn.

"We're fixing the fences."

The fencing my dad used is a row of long, slender wood stuck into the ground to prevent the horses and livestock from wandering out. The poles are slightly shorter than I am, coming up to my chest with every intention to prevent the very agile horses from thinking of them as hurdles. The last thing any of us want is for any of the horses to escape.

It had happened a while ago, and I remembered how long the men worked to gather all the horses and cows. The cows were harder to round up, no matter how many hands were helping.

I place my hands in the pockets of my overalls and examine the fence. There's nothing wrong with it, unless this isn't the spot we're supposed to be working on. The fence runs around the entire property, and our property is pretty big.

Since returning to Willow Falls, I haven't gotten the chance to explore the entire property, especially since walking isn't going to cut it. It's admirable that Grant is the one responsible for making sure that everyone on the farm does their job exactly how they're supposed to.

"The fence looks alright to me," I say and nod my head to support my claim. As if to prove what I'm saying, I reach forward and shake the fence to show Grant exactly what I'm talking about. "I don't think there's anything we can do about it. It seems stable enough."

I shake it this way and that way; it wiggles but doesn't budge much.

Grant takes a step forward and wraps his hand around mine, the very one that is shaking the pole. I stand frozen, my breath stuck. My body is buzzing while I watch the casualness of Grant's touch, how it doesn't seem to faze him that I'm unmoving by his side.

My heart is hammering loudly, trying to make sense of what is happening, trying to figure out its next course of action, and Grant holds my hand tighter like this is an everyday thing.

He lifts the pole up, his hand still wrapped around mine, and now I understand what his intention was. The pole comes out freely, like there is nothing holding it to the ground.

"That is what we are fixing," Grant says while looking at me and lets go of my hand. "Some of these poles are too loose, and we don't want any animals getting any ideas, or a horse kicking one of them down and starting something none of us would like to deal with."

I just nod my head; I'm certain I've forgotten every single thing I'm supposed to know about existing next to an ex. What does it mean if your ex holds your hand after he expresses disappointment at how things ended between you? What does it mean when you feel an electric shock through your entire body after that touch? Did he feel it too?

It'll make a good Reddit post, I decide. I'll probably end up going there for help with the way things are going for me.

I moved back to my hometown after leaving the city to clear my head. I encountered my ex, and now all these feelings are swirling inside me. P.S. What does it mean if your ex holds your hand to lift up a pole? Pole here really means pole. It isn't a euphemism for anything.

I can see all the replies now. The first one would be telling me to snap out of it and focus on getting the job done.

Looking around and clearing my throat, I asked, "So where are the poles? How are we doing this?"

Grant looks at me with a grin. "They're currently in the barn."

My jaw drops. "You want me to lift logs?"

And like it's the funniest thing in the world, the man doubles over and lets out the loudest laugh I have ever heard from him. "I don't expect you to carry them. Silas will bring them out, and we will load them on the gator and then fix them into the ground. You just have to watch us."

I frown at that. "I want to help."

"I'm not going to stop you," Grant says, handing me gloves and leaning down to say, "You look beautiful this morning, by the way."

You would think it's the first compliment I've received in my life given how hard I'm blushing. And Grant, he's the epitome of nonchalant as he spins on his heel and gets right to work on the fence.

Unsure of how to react to the compliment, I hurriedly pull on my gloves and clear my throat. I slap my cheeks lightly and shake my head to rid myself of the giddiness flowing through my veins.

I really need to learn how to accept compliments.

"First," Grant says as he pulls a new log closer to us, "we have to dig a deeper hole, and then we'll put the pole in and then cover it back up. Easy peasy."

It wasn't easy or peasy.

I feel like my back is about to split in half, and all I have done so far is dig a hole.

"That's not deep enough," Grant is quick to tell me when I start slowing down.

"I know that already," I huff out, just as I've been doing for the past few minutes—Grant is kind enough to let me know it hasn't been half an hour yet.

Don't look like such a wuss, Alexis.

A couple more minutes and the hole is complete, and despite Grant's insistence that I let him do it, I drag the pole over and place it in. I hold it up as Grant and Silas start to fill up the hole with that quick-set concrete and pat down the sand and soil on top.

"You can step away now," Grant tells me, his voice amused.

I do as I'm told, stretching out an arm as if to catch the pole if it does fall, but the pole is steady. Unmoving. To prove it, one of the other helpers shakes it a little, and when it doesn't move, they all erupt in cheers.

Grant winks and throws me a thumbs up. I grin at him, feeling thrilled.

Chapter Twelve

I finally get a break from the farm.

Well, it's not exactly a break since there's nothing left to do, but Grant has gone off to do whatever it is he does in the garage. I haven't asked him about it yet, and I'm not sure I will any time soon.

Going over to see Josie is the better choice than going over to see Grant at the garage. It's like a moth to a flame the way I keep thinking about him, and it's even worse than that because said flame is no longer in sight, and yet I'm still craving his attention.

Josie will talk some sense into me, make me see that I'm being a fool for thinking about a man from my past. My mother has been giving me side glances all afternoon, and I've been actively pretending that I'm not seeing them.

My father is also going out a lot more often, and I don't want him to worry about the farm, but it's starting to be obvious that the horse talk isn't going really well.

I make a mental note to talk to my mother about it because my father tells her everything.

Josie's café comes into sight, and I hasten my step. It's a hot day, but not so hot that it's scorching. There are a few customers sitting outside and I have no way of telling if it's because of the weather or if they're tourists hoping to enjoy the scenery.

Willow Falls is structured in a way that it has the facilities to cater to any activities or group of people. There is a museum down the street that collects rejected art by artists from the college in the next neighborhood.

The idea is to intrigue the tourists so much that they'll want to visit the next town too. I have no idea if the tactic has ever worked, since I haven't been in town long enough for it to matter.

A voice nags me about not practicing my sketches for buildings, but I quiet the voice. I'll get back to it soon, just not right now.

Right now, I push open the door to the café and the little bell jingles.

"Welcome to Josie's Café," Josie's voice rings out from the back of the store, and I smile at Minnie, Josie's mother, as she makes her way to the back of the store.

There are a lot of people in the café, and from what I can see, they're mainly just tourists. I suppose I would know more about these tourists if I would step away from the farm more often. But the truth is, I really enjoy helping out there, and if it gives my dad a break, I'm happy to do it.

Between working with Grant and making sure my mother is entertained, I haven't managed to hang out with Josie more than a quick stop for coffee and her constant trips to the farm to get more eggs or milk.

I just assumed she was baking for a show or a bake sale. I had no idea why it never occurred to me to ask.

"You're busy," I say as a way of greeting. Josie startles and turns around, holding a food basket in her hand.

"Lex, hi," Josie greets with a bright smile on her face. "We're having a sale at the market today. I'm prepping what to make for the summer fest. I thought you'd be busy, that's why I didn't bother calling. How are things on the farm?"

It's the wink Josie sends me after asking that question that lets me know that it's not such an innocent question after all.

"Why are you winking?"

Josie turns to me with a smile on her face. "You know what I mean. How are things going with Grant? Has there been anything I should know about?"

I roll my eyes as an attempt to hide the blush creeping up my face. What does Josie know? I'm starting to think that maybe coming to Josie was the wrong choice. Grant might be challenging at times, but at least he's pleasant company, and I know that he feels something for me. He also kept stealing plenty of glances at me this morning.

"I don't know what you're talking about. He's the farmhand, and I'm just helping him around the farm since my father is planning to take a step back from all the work. But I'm here now, so I can definitely help you out today."

I make a mental note to have a conversation with my father about the progress of the horse racing discussion and if he's been able to make any progress.

"How is your dad these days?"

"He's alright," I reply, accepting the little basket Josie hands me. Josie grabs the bigger basket that contains all the baked goods she hopes to sell today, and we set off together towards the market after a wave to Minnie.

"Are you really not going to tell me how things are going with Grant?"

I laugh lightly, but she can hear the nervousness in my voice. It's a fairly simple question, and I should answer it just as easily, but the truth is I don't really know how things are going with Grant.

Does he want to rekindle what we had in the past? Or is this just a fleeting moment? Did the distance wake up something in us both? Is it something worth pursuing?

What I do know is that I cannot stop thinking about him.

I don't say anything as we walk to the market to set up. Josie's stall is the first one you see when you get into the town center; she is right next to the gazebo. A lot of people have shown up to participate in the bake sale even though Josie's Café and the custom bakery are the only two in town that make and sell homemade sweets. Her baked goods sell out quickly, even before the bakery.

She supposes that everyone wants to take the opportunity to earn a little money. The question is still dancing in my head as I help Josie set up, placing different cups and lids by the napkins.

Josie places a sign that reads *Coffee and lemonade available,* even though I can't tell who in their right mind would want to take coffee in this heat. If it was in the café, I'd understand, but it's hot out, and I don't think the umbrella they have over them is going to do much.

"It's confusing," I finally say.

Josie hums to show she's listening, and I let out a sigh. If I don't talk about it with Josie, who am I going to talk about it with? And there's also the fact that part of the point of moving back to Willow Falls is to form deeper connections with people.

"I mean, he keeps bringing up all these things from our past, and I don't know how to feel about it. I want to pretend I know what's going on, but I don't really know at the end of the day. We flirt, or I think we flirt, but I'm so confused all the time. I don't know what to do."

Josie hums again, and I run my hand through my hair as a customer walks up to us with a smile on her face. I force one on my face and move to the side to give Josie room to make a sale.

The girl buys a cupcake, and Josie packs it up for her carefully and sends her off with a smile after she turns down the offer of a lemonade.

"Do you want it to mean something?"

"I don't know. I'm really confused by all of it because what if he's serious and I end up not taking it to heart? Or what if he's not serious about it and I end up taking it to heart? I feel weird around him. In a good way, of course. And I cannot stop thinking about him."

"You could talk to him about it."

"Oh yeah, why didn't I think of that? 'Hey, Grant, seeing as I'm in town, and even though I don't know what I'm doing here yet—if I want to stay or leave—do you have feelings for me?' yeah right Josie, that sounds terrible."

"You plan on leaving?"

"I quit my job on a whim, and I miss creating. I haven't drawn anything since I got back, and I don't want to lose my touch at being able to draw buildings. The thing is I think I want to go back, but I don't want to do the whole bone-crushing way of living. You know? I loved my job, just not where I was. What if I can't find my place after this?"

Josie nods her head like she knows, but the movement is so slow that I doubt that she knows.

"I think the thing about Willow Falls is that we all think that we can come back after a burn out, experience the good weather, stay with the familiar faces, and then we can up and leave again. I did the same thing, you know. Just like you did, the city was draining me, and I thought I'd come back during my leave, spend time with my mom, and then pack up and go back to this normal, fulfilling life in the city.

You haven't been back for a long while, and this thing with Grant doesn't have to be a big thing. And trust me, Grant can take care of himself. You don't have to promise him the entire world; you just need to see where this tide takes you."

I consider this and nod my head. It's solid advice. "Have you always been this smart or..."

Josie moves like she's going to shove me, but she pauses and looks past me. "Speak of the devil."

I spin around to see Grant striding towards us, looking like a daydream. It's insane how hot someone can look in a simple t-shirt and jeans. "What is he doing here?"

"It's like he can't stay away," Josie says, winking, not hiding the way she's gawking at Grant.

"Hey ladies," Grant greets with a smile on his face. "I haven't seen you in a minute, Josie."

"I hear you've been busy showing our dearest Alexis here all the ropes she'll need to pull off working on the farm."

I elbow Josie, who just puts on a smile.

Grant just smiles. "I came to satisfy my sweet tooth today since we're taking a break."

He's looking at me now, a smile on his face like he knows something I don't. He probably thinks I'm bad at maintaining eye contact, but it's the sun that's making it hard to look him in the eyes, especially since he looks so dreamy. But seriously, his eyes are perfect.

"How's Lex as a student?" Josie says as she puts a cookie and a cupcake in a paper box as if she already knows what the man is going to order.

"Oh, she's stubborn," Grant says with a nod of his head. "Never listens to what I tell her, and she takes every word that comes out of my mouth as a challenge or a diss. Really, there's no in-between. But it keeps me on my toes."

Josie's laugh is loud, and I'm affronted both by Grant's reply and by Josie's response to it.

"I can't believe the both of you. Are you ganging up on me?"

"Nope, I'm just reporting to a concerned friend. But she did a good job fixing up the fence."

I groan further and wish there was a hole I could bury myself in.

"Alright, you two," Josie says and waves us away. "Off you go."

"What?" I protest before I can think too much about it, "I was going to spend the entire day with you."

Josie rolls her eyes. "Go around and try some other person's treat or something. Enjoy this while it lasts."

I assume Grant is no longer looking our way because Josie winks at me and makes a shooing motion. When I turn around to look at Grant, he's looking at me with a glow, and that is all the convincing I need to go with him.

I'm in trouble.

Chapter Thirteen

"I thought you'd be at the garage." I say.

Grant leads us through the market, smiling and greeting all the locals. A couple of kids run past us, and I just smile. The smell of freshly baked goods mixes perfectly with the air and settles lightly in my stomach.

It fills me with an emotion that doesn't threaten to drown me. Even with Grant walking slowly beside me, chewing the cookie he got from Josie with a look of contentment on his face, I don't want to run and hide.

"I was at the garage, but there weren't a lot of jobs that the other guys couldn't handle, so I decided to take a break and come see what the market has to offer, and here you are."

I nod in understanding. "So, you just showed up."

"I may or may not have gone back to the farm to get some work done and your mother told me you headed to the bake sale with Josie. I took the liberty to come see you outside of your overalls. Even if you do look really good in them," he says with a wink.

I've never felt that exposed in my yellow flower-patterned dress. It was a last-minute purchase from a time I assumed a coworker was going to ask me out on a date. It didn't work out; the coworker was just too friendly and managed to get a transfer out of the state before I could embarrass myself further.

"Well, good thing I brought this dress then."

UGH, why did I say that?

Grant laughs loudly; it's a melodious sound that warms my cheeks and makes me take a sip of the lemonade Josie handed me at the last minute.

"It's been a while since I saw you in a dress. You look really beautiful today."

"So, what do I look like on other days?"

Grant looks at me with wide eyes, like he didn't expect my reply to come so swiftly. He opens his mouth and closes it with no sound escaping. Then finally, he says, "You know I didn't mean anything by that. You look beautiful every day, I have to mentally prepare myself to not lose my head each morning."

A smile breaks on my face. "That's sweet. You don't look so bad yourself most days."

Looking over at him, I nudge him with my shoulder.

Grant laughs at that, and I want to take it back. I want to tell him that he looks really handsome, and the early evening light is hitting him right and making his skin look like he's a god. The glint of the sun hits his irises perfectly. Looking at him is like a daydream.

But I don't say anything as we make our way out of the market and towards my parents' house. It's like our youth all over again, and I have to fight the skip in my step.

"Look who it is," Jeremy Dexter calls as we walk past the barber shop. "It's Willow Falls's own couple of the year. Most likely to get married to each other, was it?"

If my cheeks weren't red before, they're on fire now.

"Hey Jeremy," Grant calls out. "How's it going?"

Jeremy rushes over to us and does a very complicated bro shake with Grant. "I haven't seen you around, man. How's the garage doing? I'd like to come over sometime, but my old man is unable to stick by the shop these days, so I'm doing all the work myself."

"That's alright," Grant says with a light smile. "How's your father doing?"

"He's old," Jeremy says, like it's that easy, and I can't help the snort that escapes me, and like always, like a shark drawn to blood, Jeremy turns his attention to me.

"Hey, Miss Pretty Thing."

For someone who just reminded us that we were voted most likely to get married, he doesn't care for Grant's presence.

"Hey Jeremy," I greet with a smile of my own.

"How are you finding Willow Falls? Do you need me to show you around any?"

"Hey," Grant says and pulls Jeremy away from me. "I thought you were over your crush on her. You said so."

"Until I saw her," Jeremy replies with a wink in my direction. "If you decide you don't want him anymore, I'm always here for you."

I laugh and roll my eyes. "Say hello to your father for me."

Jeremy grins and runs back to the shop as a customer heads in. He waves goodbye and we turn and walk away as quickly as we can.

Heading back to the farm, our conversation carried on.

"He's still the funniest person I've ever met."

"You think he's funnier than me?"

It's my turn to speak, and Grant laughs at my discomfort. "I'm just joking. I always found his crush on you hilarious because it's always hard to tell if he's serious or not."

We keep walking, the silence between us is comfortable, our hands brushed against each other. But I can't seem to forget Jeremy's comment about mine and Grant's relationship. Grant is making no move to bring it up, and I feel like if I don't mention it now, we might never get a chance to talk about it again.

And the truth is I want to know all about it. If Grant still thinks about us. If, like me, he tried to push back the memories so it wouldn't hurt so much. Instead of thinking about it anymore, I decide to blurt it out and worry about the consequences later.

"I can't believe the whole school voted us most likely to get married," I say, hoping that my voice isn't giving away how nervous I am.

Grant laughs, and I realize that it's not the first time I've heard him laugh today. He's been laughing at everything I've been saying, and I know for a fact that I'm not that funny.

"I mean, we did make one hell of a couple. You were the school's most likely to succeed, whereas I was voted most likely to not make it out of Willow Falls."

I frown. "I don't remember you being voted for that. I do remember that you were voted most likely to become mayor."

"It's kind of the same thing."

"Not really. Everyone thought you were going to make the town great, and to be honest, you're kind of doing a fantastic job at it. Why did you leave the city, though? I remember that everyone said you got a job there, and it was a big deal."

Grant whistles. "You were asking about me during your return trips?"

"Well, I had to. I didn't know what you were up to, and there was no way of finding out. My mother didn't talk about you unless she was asked. I didn't keep contact with Josie when I left either."

"You really did cut everyone off, huh?"

"I wouldn't call it that. It sounds bad when you put it in those words."

"Because it was. We were friends more than we were a couple. I thought at the very least, you were going to give me an explanation, but you stopped taking my calls. You may have managed to focus just fine after you decided I wasn't worth your time, but I'd like you to know that it was torture for me. I was hell bent on coming over to see you, but it didn't even seem like it would be worth it."

I kick rocks with my foot. I have no good response to that, and it's easy to see how hurt Grant was by my decision. If I could take it back, would I? I managed to achieve all of my dreams, which meant that cutting off Grant did work to that effect, but everything after that was a failure. Did he really think we were more friends than anything?

I got lonely and there was no one to call. My parents were there, but I didn't want to bother them, so I always pretended that I was hanging out with friends even though my face was buried in a book while the world raged on.

Now, looking back, as we make a turn away from the main entrance to the farm to the side entrance, I think that it would have been nice to skip a class or two for no reason. It would have been nice to get drunk for the hell of it. I'm realizing a lot now.

We make it back to the farm, and I follow Grant as he leads me toward the wildflower field. My heart hammers in my chest, and I take small breaths to calm myself down. Back in the day I had to sneak out here because my parents, despite being cool now and trying to get me with him, were overly strict and would have killed me if they found out that I was sneaking out to meet a boy.

"It was lonely," I admit, because what else is there to say? "It was so fucking lonely."

We're standing in the field now, under the large oak tree, and I look down at the slope where the fields run down and blend into the other property. The family who owned that land sold it to Dad a few years back, but he hasn't done anything with it just yet.

"I spent most nights wondering if you were out with friends, if you'd found someone new, if it was easier for you. I wanted to call, you have no idea how badly I wanted to reach out and say I was sorry, but I talked myself out of it every time because I didn't want to be selfish."

"You should've been selfish. I was miserable and I waited and waited. I reached out and hoped that you'd see how persistent I was and that it would change something for you."

I don't say anything, I don't even turn to look at him. What does one say to something like that?

"Lex," Grant says and nudges me until I look at him. When our eyes meet, my breath catches in my throat. He is much closer to me than I thought.

Grant's eyes are pretty, and under the setting sun, he looks absolutely divine, like his eyes are the mirror with which I'm to view the world. As weak as I am, I let my eyes roam all over his face, exerting extra strength to not look at his lips.

But Grant seems determined, especially to see me break. He leans closer to me and I forget to breathe. I'm stuck between an inhale and an exhale, and my chest tightens with the effort.

"It's always been you for me," is all Grant says before he's leaning in.

His breath hits my lips and I swallow, shocked I didn't choke. His lips are so close to mine, and my eyes flutter, trying to close and give in to this moment. There's no good reason to not give in, so I surrender myself to it. I lean in, our lips touch, and just as I'm about to put my arms around his neck, someone yells.

"Alexis!" My eyes fly open. "Your mother fell down the stairs. She's hurt."

Chapter Fourteen

A few days have passed, and as if she can sense that I'm in a bad mood, Aster accepts the sugar cubes I offer her and nuzzles into my hand before pulling away. It's not enough to put a smile on my face, but it warms my heart just a little.

My mother fractured her ankle, and even though she insists she's fine, the doctor has ordered her to not do anything stressful. This is the most worried my father has ever been, and he doesn't need any more stress.

Apparently, my mother tried to do some laundry, a task that I had taken over doing because the laundry room is downstairs and dad doesn't want her taking unnecessary trips up and down the poorly lit stairs even if Mom calls it exercise. But for some reason, she got it in her head to do the laundry herself.

Look where exercising has gotten her.

With my mother indisposed and my father worried sick, I had to take on more responsibilities with the farm. Which means I've been working more hours, taking more trips to deliver goods to customers who can't make it to the farm to get them.

Grant has offered to help out, but I feel a sense of pride for these things. I want to be able to achieve something without Grant helping me. Even if I feel overwhelmed, I want to be able to do what my parents are doing without someone hovering over me thinking I can't get the job done.

His heart is in a good place, but I don't know how to accept the help he's offering. I'm not stupid, I recognize it as one of the aftereffects of working in a company that liked to take credit for the littlest thing, the way it forced me to depend entirely on myself because even when I let someone help me, they always managed to mess things up for me.

I loathe the fact that even after leaving the city to come back to Willow Falls, I still haven't managed to shake off that aftereffect. It's killing me, even more that I've brushed off all of Grant's attempts to talk to me and comfort me.

This is something that I need to go through alone, and it'll be better as soon as my mother is back on her feet. But the journey thus far has been trying. I seem to be failing in every direction. The hens pecked on my hand when I went to get their eggs. I was chased by a cow relentlessly, and everyone watched me scream at the top of my lungs as I tried to get away from it. Little did I know this cow just had a calf. And when I managed to escape it—one of the farmhands managed to gain control of the cow—I got chased down by one of the turkeys and then tripped over a shovel.

All in all, it felt like all of the animals on the farm were putting their heads together to reject me as a helper. None of them were giving me a chance to get to know them or to take care of them. It's like they can feel the stress buzzing off of me.

All of this makes me want to both retreat to my shell and to try harder to gain their trust. It's stressing me out even more. But despite all of that, at least there is Aster, who is nuzzling my hand like I am worth something.

I want to pull this beautiful horse to my chest and press a kiss to her brown fur. I want to braid her mane and add ribbons to it. Make a worldwide presentation on my Instagram: 'Meet Aster, the only one on my side.'

Maybe I shouldn't have quit my job. I should've taken the raise and carried on suffering for a couple more years. The very thought of it makes me shudder. That is a cruel thing to wish on myself.

Tomorrow will be a better day.

"Figured I'd find you here."

Aster raises her head at the intrusion, but I don't look away from or stop petting her. Grant's hand comes into my line of sight and ruffles Aster's mane. And there is a reason why animals shouldn't be fully trusted because

Aster softly neighs at the affection and nuzzles into Grant's hand.

Grant's chuckle is light, and I have to struggle to push back my scoff. A couple of seconds pass between us. My body is still thrumming from the mortification that while I was lip locking with Grant, my mother was screaming in agony.

"Are you okay?" Grant asks, and I can tell that he's not looking at me. He's still pretending that Aster is the most fascinating thing in the room. I won't do anything to call him out on it.

"I'm fine. It's nothing I can't handle."

"That's not what I'm asking," Grant says, and this time, he then turns his attention to me. "Come on, look at me."

I resist until Grant reaches out and physically turns me to look at him. I don't quite look at him even then, afraid of what his eyes are going to tell me. Grant lets out a sigh, and I try not to take it to heart.

"Why are you being so stubborn, Alexis? Just look at me and tell me what's wrong."

"Nothing is wrong," I say, and this time I make sure to look him in the eyes. Immediately, I regret it and fight the urge to look away. Grant's eyes search mine to find something, but if there's one thing I've mastered over the years of working with and for Greg Jr., it is how to mask my emotions and wipe my eyes of anything that is going to give me away.

"Alexis."

"You already know this hasn't been the best week for me. My mother is hurt, and on top of that, my father has to pull back a bit. And I can't help him with whatever negotiations he's making. But that's nothing new, you already know that."

"I just want to know how you're doing, there is no need to be snappy with me."

"I'm not being snappy with you," I start and pause when I hear the way my voice sounds, tight and dismissive. "This isn't a good time, Grant. I'd rather not talk."

Grant snorts at that, and I'm affronted by his audacity. How dare he find humor in what we're talking about. What about this whole situation is funny to him?

"What's funny?"

"You."

"Excuse me?"

"I mean, I don't know why I thought anything would have changed since the last time we spoke to each other. Not talking has always been your strong suit, and yet, somehow, I imagined that it was because of the distance, and if we were in the same place together, it would be easier to get you to trust me.

I'm not trying to control you or whatever you think is going to happen if you tell me how you're feeling without holding back. I do care about you. When I ask, it's because I want to make sure you're doing okay. I want to make sure that you know that you're not alone through all of this. And you keep shutting me out and keeping me at arm's length."

I heave and try to calm myself down, but the man in front of me is breathing hard too, like he's run a million miles. Is that how I come across to him? I don't want him to think that I'm keeping him at arm's length, but I can see it now.

However, it's unfair for Grant to bring our past into it. How would he feel if I were to do the same? I wrack my brain for something to say in accusation of him and in defense of myself and my actions, but my brain comes up with nothing.

Grant has always been nothing but nice to me, open with me too. I want to take it all back, but it feels like losing, and I've lost a lot of myself these last few years. I'm not going to lose anymore.

"I'm fine," I say instead, and stand tall. "You would know if you took the time to listen to what I've been saying. I'm doing alright, and there's no need for me to lean on you because it makes no sense to do so if I'm not in need of it. How about you just—"

At that moment Grant grabs my face and pulls me closer to him.

He says, "What?"

I purse my lips to stop the words from falling out. There is so much I shouldn't say, and I'm not going to be an idiot and blurt it out. I feel so warm around him, but this isn't the time.

I grab his hands from my face.

"Listen, Grant, I appreciate your concern. I really do, but I really can't do this right now."

"I just want to know how you're doing. You're not alone, Wildflower. You can rely on me. I'm here for you."

I nod my head because it's easier than fighting against him. I'd rather not fight him at all. "I appreciate that. And if I ever need to, I'll reach out to you. I know it seems like I'm going through a lot, but I have a plan to get through this."

"You're going to leave, aren't you?"

It's the way Grant says it, like he's already figured it out and he's just putting it out there to give me a chance to deny it. I bite my cheek, unsure of how to respond to the accusation. It's unfair of Grant to spring it on me when I'm in the middle of spiraling. What if I haven't even made up my mind yet?

"Fuck," Grant says and runs his hand through his hair. "I mean, I sort of assumed that you were just back in town to cool off, but then I heard you talking about quitting your job, and I figured, especially since you started taking on jobs on the farm, that you'd want to stay, but this whole time your heart wasn't in it, was it?"

"I don't know, Grant," I whisper, the most honest I have been tonight. "I really don't know whether I want to stay or leave. I've just been trying to figure things out."

"And the backup plan was to leave at the end of the day. Why do you never talk to me about these things? Why do you keep trying to make decisions about us by yourself?"

I open my mouth to explain, to defend myself, to make him see what it's like for me, but still, no words manage to make it out of my mouth. I'm trying hard to hold back these tears welling up.

Where is this all coming from?

Grant nods his head and runs his hand through his hair again. "I see how it is."

He turns around and walks out of the stable, his shoulders slightly slumped.

"Us," I whisper to Grant's back as I watch him leave, unable to call him back, unsure of what to say to make him stay.

Chapter Fifteen

"You're fussing," my mother says as I try to fluff the throw pillow on the seat she's on. "It's just a fracture; my hands still work fine, and I can fluff my own pillows."

As if to prove her point, the pillow is dragged out of my hands, and my mother glares at me. "Get out of here, sweetie."

"I need to make sure everything's in order," I say and pick up the book my mother's book club will be discussing. I scrunch my nose as I read the title. *The Mafia's Bride.* "Do you ever read anything intellectual?"

"Do you ever, I don't know, leave the house? Since we're talking now, why don't you tell me why you're avoiding Grant? Did you two have a fight?"

"What?" The inflection of the word is enough for my mother to raise her brows.

"Is that why you're both moping around?"

"I'm not moping."

Ok, *of course* I'm moping.

"Right. So, he's the only one moping?" My mother nudges her head towards the window and I'm forced to look in that direction. Outside the window, Grant is watching the horses graze and the forlorn look on his face is obvious.

I turn around, ignoring the ache in my chest and look at my mother. "He looks fine to me."

My mother nods like she does when she doesn't quite believe what I'm saying, but she doesn't want to make an issue out of it.

"What's the problem? You can talk to me about it."

"It's.... nothing."

"Alexis, sit."

"There's really no need for this, everything is fine. And besides, your friends will be here soon, so you need to get ready. I'll bring out the drinks and snacks."

"Sit down."

My mother's voice is firm, and it's conditioning more than anything that makes me take the seat next to her. From my position, I can see Grant through the window, him watching the horses while looking like a daydream.

I'm screwed.

I divert my gaze away from him when he turns back to the house, like he can feel my gaze on him, but I know he's too far away to be able to get a glimpse inside the house. Still, I would rather not push my luck.

For the longest time, neither of us say anything, just watching Grant outside the window, who true to my mother's words, is moping.

"Did you fight?"

"A disagreement."

"You want to tell me what it was about?"

I close my eyes to gather my thoughts. "I don't know what I want. It's like we're on different pages."

My mother makes a noise that sounds like it's coming from the back of her throat, but I don't open my eyes. I need to close my eyes to be able to do this.

"I know you remember we went to prom together, but it was more than that. We were dating."

My mother scoffs now. "It wasn't as much a secret as you think, Lex. You used to sneak out all the time to meet him by the fields. Your father always wanted to chase after you and drag you back, but I always managed to convince him to leave you be. You're a smart girl, but you didn't think about the cameras we have for the animals."

I don't feel shocked that my mother knows. I remember the coy looks she used to send my way the morning after meeting Grant. Back then, I thought she was being funny, but now, it makes more sense.

"Well, we were dating and while in college we tried to make it work, but I just wasn't able to manage it. I was sad in college, Mom," I say for the first time. "It was horrible. I just wasn't able to make friends. Here in Willow Falls, we made friends by proximity, but in college, I had to figure out who wanted to be friends with me. I had to go out with them, and sometimes, they just decided they didn't want to be friends with me anymore."

My mother's hand covers mine, and I swallow back the tears, grateful that she's letting me talk about it.

"I wasn't sure how to navigate that, and on top of that, I was struggling with school. It took me a long time to grasp concepts. I wasn't the intelligent girl that left Willow Falls. College courses, plus the new environment, were a lot to handle. Between all of that and all the calls we were making back and forth to make our relationship work, it was taking a toll on me, so I figured that if I was having a hard time, it wasn't enough reason to drag Grant down with me."

My mother makes the same noise again, and I'm quick to defend myself.

"It wasn't just him, though; I stopped reaching out to everyone, including Josie. Josie got the message easily, but Grant was harder to shake off. He called repeatedly, and I decided to not take the calls or reply to the messages. Eventually I forgot to even check if he had reached out."

"Alexis," my mother breathes out. "You can't make that type of decision for the both of you."

"I know that, but I just thought it was the right thing to do. And the truth is I got tired of hearing about his day. He had friends and was out doing fun things while my life remained monotonous. The same routine, and even though he didn't say it, I could feel the sadness he felt for me, pity even. It was horrible, Mom."

My mother squeezes my hand, and I fight the tears again. I take a deep breath to steady myself. This is really not what I thought I'd be doing today, but here I am pouring my heart out to my mother.

"We've been getting along since I got back, but there is still the uncertainty of my being here. I don't know if I want to stay or if I want to go back and work. And Grant, he feels betrayed about my lack of decision. He thinks I'm being cruel by being uncertain, but I genuinely don't know. I am so confused on why I am feeling this way towards him, but also so confused on what is right for me."

My mother hums. "I see how this is hard for the both of you, but you need to talk to him at some point, Alexis. Whether you choose to stay in Willow Falls or go back to work in the city, it's something you need to talk about. The last time you left town, you didn't talk to him for over a decade. Don't blame the man for worrying that if he lets you leave again, you'll cut him off for good."

"I don't want to promise something I'm not certain I can give. What if I get tired of being here? This town is only lively now because it's summer and a lot of tourists are choosing to relax here. Other than that, we don't really get a lot of traffic around these parts. I'm used to the hustle and bustle of city life. What if I stay and then we don't work out? What do I do then?"

"Whether you leave or stay, that's hardly the point," my mother says. "You need to figure out if you want him in the picture or not. He's open to being with you and ensuring this thing between the both of you doesn't fade away again. The problem isn't with him and what he wants, it's with you and how willing you are to let yourself want him. There's more to this town than what happens during the summer. Don't forget about the Winter fest."

I open my mouth to argue with my mother, to say something in my defense, but a knock comes on the door. And without even waiting, the door is shoved open and two ladies make their way into the house, a basket in one hand and the horrendous book in the other hand.

"Alexis," they say at the same time, a smile on their faces as they take me in. "You're even prettier now that we've seen you up close."

"You should come to the house sometime; my son is going to be thrilled to see you," my mom's friend Mary says.

"I think my grandson is going to be perfect for you," Louise counters, eying her friend for daring to mention her son.

"Do you have a boyfriend?"

"Are things with Jonah's boy serious? People are say-ing they've been seeing the both of you all over town."

I get to my feet, overwhelmed by the attention and unsure of how to respond to the question. "I'm going to go outside and help Grant with the animals. If you need anything, you can holler."

"Grant is Jonah's boy," my mother explains to the ladies. "Remember he's helping out on the farm?"

The women buzz in response, and as I slip out of the house, I hear them congratulating my mother for taking the initiative to bring Grant into their house. As if my mother has done it to trap the man as opposed to offering him the job because she needed the help.

I know my mother isn't going to correct her friends, she's going to let them carry on this belief that it is her intention for the both of us to end up together.

Instead of heading to Grant like I said I would, I make a turn and head out of the farm. I can't face Grant now, not after everything that was said and unsaid. Seeing him would require me to clarify a lot of things, and I'm not even sure I understood any of it myself.

My body itches to be away from this town, and my legs want to run as far as I can but doing that will only serve to confirm Grant's accusation. Even though there's evidence that supports his claims.

I've been sending out applications and trying to get my portfolio out there. No one is getting back to me, which is weird because I do have the experience, and all the buildings I've worked on are well rated.

The magazines I've appeared in are supposed to give me an edge, but either no one has opened my application, or they have and they don't care about it.

A walk will clear my head.

Chapter Sixteen

I wake up early the next morning. Well before anyone in the house .

I go about my chores with the type of focus that only shows up when I'm trying to bring out the best building in my mind. I pay attention to the cows, patting them to show my support, filling their water basins. Dropping alfalfa cubes for them before I move on.

The hens come next. With the number of experiences I've had, I can pretend to be something of an expert. The hens don't peck me anymore as their eggs are taken away, like they've accepted me as one of their own. I bend down to pat a few as they gather at my feet. This gold one in particular always looks up at me like she understands my struggle.

Then it's back to the house to brew coffee before rushing upstairs to get ready. By the time I make it back down, the rest of the farm has woken up, including my mother.

There's coffee in my mother's hand as she grabs the basket of eggs I collected this morning.

"Good morning," I greet her, placing a light kiss on her cheeks.

My mother smiles, taking her eyes off the basket to look at me as she pours herself more coffee.

"Where's Dad?" I ask, ignoring the searching look she is throwing my way.

"He should be down soon. You're dressed up. Why?"

I wouldn't call a pair of jeans and a plain t-shirt dressed up. But with the jacket I have on, I can see why my outfit is out of the ordinary, especially given what I've been wearing for the past couple of days.

"I think I'm going to go with Dad today, see what it's like to shadow him."

My mother takes a sip of her coffee with a hum. I know what she's thinking, but I didn't spend all of last night giving myself a pep talk to let a little observation from my mother's eyes wear me down.

"Is there any specific reason you're going with him?"

"I just want to try my hand at something else. All the helping around the farm is tiring me out, and maybe looking at a new scenery is going to help me. Plus, I need to know what's going on with the horses."

I don't mention that the past week has been hell for me. The silence between Grant and I has been tense, the both of us waiting for the other person to say something and break the silence. I would like Grant to apologize for blowing up on me like that. I suppose that he would also like me to apologize for something, but I'm not sure what I am supposed to say or not say. I guess I don't blame him, though.

My mother nods her head like the excuse makes sense. "And this has nothing to do with Grant then?"

"Not everything is about a man, Mom," I say, taking a big gulp of my coffee. An action I regret immediately because it's still very hot.

Ouch.

I turn around hastily to the sink and spit out the liquid in my mouth. I take the chance to dump the coffee as well because I've lost the desire to drink it.

My mother chuckles and shakes her head as if she didn't just witness her daughter burn her tongue. "So, if I suggest that you take Grant with you, that would be alright?"

"Why would we take him with us? Who's going to help you with the farm?"

"My ankle is fine," she replies, and as if to prove her point, she lifts her leg and shakes it in my direction as if to say, *see.* "Plus, Silas is here with the other boys today."

I'm about to reply when my father comes into the kitchen with a smile on his face. Like he does every morning, he heads to my mom first and places a light kiss on her forehead as if they didn't wake up in the same bed.

It feels almost nauseating even though I wouldn't mind having this type of love for myself one day.

I pour my father a cup of coffee. "I'm coming with you today."

He's quiet for a couple of seconds before he replies, and even though I don't see him, I'm certain he looks at my mother first. "What?"

"I want to come with you and see how the discussion with the horses is going."

"Aren't you supposed to be working on the farm today? With Grant? What happened to that plan?"

"She went ahead and did what she considered her own share of the work," my mother says and gestures to the basket of eggs sitting before them.

My father watches the basket for a while, saying nothing and sipping his coffee.

"I want a change of scenery."

And I *need* a change today.

My father dips his head in understanding, still looking at the basket like it holds the answer he's looking for. "You can come with me. I'm certain I will appreciate the company. And maybe when they see you, they would want to speed up the discussion. The event is in a couple of weeks, and I know that more farms are starting to put in their offer. We desperately need the money, so I'm hoping that something will change today."

I frown. "If the farm needs money, you guys know that—"

"No," my mother is quick to say. My father is also shaking his head.

This isn't the first time that I've offered to put my money into the farm, but my parents are always against the idea. I have no idea why they would choose to keep seeking funds when I have no problem providing the money they need.

"I don't mind."

"You should spend the money on yourself."

"I really don't need anything. You can even consider it an investment into the farm if it's too much for you to just take the money from me."

"You worked hard for that money."

"And I'm saying that I can give it to you if you need it. If the farm needs it. I want to invest in the farm, it shouldn't be that much of a big deal. That's my name on that barn too."

My parents go quiet, and I wonder if I've managed to get across to them. They look at each other and have that communication they always do with their eyes. I wish that I could have this with Grant. Or do I already, and I've missed the signs?

The thought startles me and makes me stand taller. Until now, the man of my dreams has always been faceless, but now, he's taking a figure, a shape, a face. Grant?

I shake my head. It must be the proximity. There's no way your first love is your "meant to be."

"We don't want to be dependent on you."

"Accepting money from me when you need it is not being dependent on me; it's making a good business decision. We can even talk to your lawyer and have him draw up an agreement for us."

The suggestion makes both of them nod in agreement, and I sigh in relief. I know my parents are stubborn, but this is the worst of it.

"If we lose the chance to use our horses at the next race, we'll take the help you offer. But until then, we'll just have our lawyers draw something up. Although I'm certain that we will win the contract, we always do."

We don't win the contract. As I drive us home, my father is silent in the passenger seat. I have no idea what to say to calm him down or assure him. I can tell that he genuinely thought he was going to be the one to provide the horses, and that's because their farm has always been given that honor.

"They say Aster is too old now, and they should give the chance to someone else. A colt perhaps."

I don't know what to say to that. I don't think that Aster is old, but she's been around even since Daisy was alive. My parents got her during Daisy's last days, and since then she's always been the horse that the first rider got on once she was saddle trained. I honestly only know this because I came home for memorial day weekend when they were training her.

It was an honor my family didn't joke about.

"We were going to get another horse. The other horses, they're fine specimens too, you know. But they're not as fast as they used to be and too old for breeding. A lot of racers who use them only do so because they're used to them. It's only a matter of time before we'd be prohibited from showing up with them."

"If it was this bad, why didn't any of you tell me? I don't have a lot of things to do with my money. Especially since my apartment is paid for and I'm alone."

"You're going to start a family someday," my father starts, but I'm quick to cut him off.

"And I'll still have enough. I work, Dad. I don't sit around doing nothing. If you don't want to take the money, you could have asked me to consider investing so you could get some new horses. We've always had the best horses, and if our horses were up to standard, you wouldn't have had to be going on all these trips. These people would have come to you."

"We thought Aster still had a bright future ahead of her. We figured if she got selected this time, it could be her last public experience, and then we could get new horses from the payment we'll get, but that has gone to hell now."

I don't reply, I just focus on the road, doing my best to loosen my grip on the steering wheel.

"Your mother is going to be so disappointed."

I nod in silent agreement, my mother is really going to be heartbroken, but my parents are so attuned to one another, that they'll try their best to comfort each other thinking the other person is sadder than them.

It'll be something to watch.

"It's going to be alright," I say as I squeeze my father's hand. He looks away from the window to smile at me. I keep my hand on his, taking it away to switch gears. I'd offer for us to eat somewhere, but I can tell my father is desperate to get home to my mom and get comfort from her. Plus, Randy, the farmhand we took along with us, has a prior engagement.

So, I focus on the road and start to wonder if I can stay in Willow Falls. And if I stay, is this something I can experience with Grant? The answer doesn't come to me.

There's someone standing on the front porch when we pull up the drive. No, that's wrong. Grant is standing on the front porch with someone familiar. I immediately feel sick to my stomach as I bring the car to a stop. The man is wearing a grey suit and clutching a suitcase in his hands.

I know exactly who it is just by the way he's standing. My stomach dips when I notice my mother sitting on the porch too.

My father is out of the car and he's walking to the house. He doesn't exactly stop to question the man; instead, he stops in front of Grant, and Grant must say something because my father tilts his head and pats him on his back.

He says hello to the other man, who nods, his greeting quick and furious. I take a deep breath to steady myself. Grant and I are still at odds due to the conversation about staying or leaving Willow Falls.

What is he going to think about the man standing next to him? Greg Jr.'s personal secretary sighs in relief the second I step out of the car. He hurries over to me like he can't wait to get away from Grant.

I don't pay attention to the man who's approaching me. I keep my eyes on Grant, and he's also looking right back at me. Even though I have no idea what Greg's secretary, Samuel, is about to say, I can tell it's not something that's going to put a smile on my face.

Not just because he's from my former company, but because Grant is looking at me like he's trying to see a different reaction on my face, something other than the one he was already used to, and I don't know what I'm supposed to offer to him.

My parents head inside the house, giving the three of us space, and I want to go with them, offer them comfort, but before then, I have to address the man standing next to me, the one who is waiting for me to fix my attention on him so he can deliver the message.

"Ms. Larson, thank God you came home. I have a message from the boss, Senior," he hands me an envelope and I look away from Grant to take it from him. "He wants you back at work. The details are in the letter."

My head snaps up to look at him. He's wide eyed, staring at me. When I look over to where Grant is standing, I'm met with his retreating back. The words I need to call him back die in my throat.

Chapter Seventeen

Samuel Becket is Greg Jr.'s personal secretary. Before he showed up and stayed, Greg Jr. was going through secretaries like they were travel-sized soaps. I had never seen anyone gain and lose a secretary that many times. It was insane to witness.

Then Samuel showed up and persisted until Greg Jr. had no choice but to keep him on. If there was one person Greg Jr. trusted in the company, it was Samuel. The man was trained by the same secretary who used to work for his father. While everyone assumed Greg Sr. would let his secretary continue with his son, he said he saw no reason why the man who started working when he did won't retire with him.

It's one of the things that make me hold Greg Sr. in high esteem, but be that as it may, it was enough reason for him to send someone over to my hometown, my house, to ask me to come back to work.

It isn't Samuel's presence that I hate, it is the fact that he sat with Grant and, without a doubt, talked about me. I know Samuel enough to know that he can strike up a conversation with even the most unwilling participant. I've seen it happen time and time again, and if he had a conversation with Grant, then without a doubt he told Grant the same thing he told me.

Which isn't even a good thing to begin with.

"What are you doing here, Samuel?"

He looks surprised by my question. "I told you already. Greg Sr. called and nearly tore down the entire company when he found out that you were gone. Greg Jr. isn't happy that his father came to work to tear him a new one because of you, but I've managed to talk to and calm him down. I'm sure you're pleased to know that."

"I quit. Wasn't that enough for them to understand?"

"Yes, I saw. I was there. We lost that contract, by the way, if it means anything to you, which I'm certain it does. Greg Jr. wasn't able to make the presentation, but that's only because you left in a hurry and left him no time to get ready. It threw all of us off, and the clients were not pleased. And during the time it took to convince them to give us another chance, the boss has been trying to bring you back, but you've done nothing but turn him down."

"I meant it when I left, I'm not just going to go back because you're asking. That job took too much from me, and you were there to see it all."

Samuel nods his head in agreement. "I felt inspired to leave once, but I actually do like my job. And Greg Jr. has given me an increase in salary almost like he's scared that I would do something stupid and quit. I think I have you to thank for that."

"I'm not coming back."

Samuel sighs. "Are you just not going to work again? You don't even know what I'm trying to offer you here. You're a really good architect, one of the best. Taking a break is fine, but the idea that you're never going to design a building again is doing a great disservice not just to yourself but to the world. You can't just stop."

I don't know what to say in response to that. I know I'm a good architect. That's not something that I've ever doubted, but no one has ever said that not putting my work out there is a great disservice to the world.

And hearing it from the one person in that godforsaken building who knew exactly what I had to put up with fills me with so much joy I nearly ask what it is Greg Sr. is offering.

"I want to keep designing, but I don't want to do it in a space that is suffocating. Samuel, you know it was hell for me; why would I want to continue in that environment?"

"You're making my job really difficult, and I thought we liked each other."

I glare at him.

"You should have told me you wanted to leave, I would have tried to get you something. I have good connections; you have no idea."

I grin at him. "Honestly, I had no idea I was going to leave until I quit. It was just too much. But I like it here. It somehow gives me a sense of peace right now."

Samuel looks around before turning his attention back to me with his nose scrunched up. "You like it on the farm?"

"Hey, I grew up here. And yes, I love it ."

"I mean, I see the vision, especially with the grumpy hunk over there," Samuel says and jerks his head backward in the direction that Grant has disappeared. "Anyone with eyes would want this life. I thought he was going to bash my head in. The second he found out we used to work together, the friendliness he was showering me with disappeared. I mean, he still tried his best to be nice, but it was so obvious he wanted me to leave before you came back. One would think I was trying to steal you from him."

I laugh too loud and too forcefully for it not to be anything but suspicious. Samuel turns to me with raised brows.

"No, the both of you? Alexis!"

"There's nothing there."

"You say that now, but I was nearly herded out like cattle. I should be heading back, but you hang on to this so the higher-ups will think I was able to talk you down a notch. I want to still feel indispensable. On the other hand, I'll try to see if I can get you something remote. So, you'll still feel close to your boy toy."

"It's not like that."

Samuel lets out a hmmm and crosses over to the other side of the road, and seeing it for the first time, the silver sports car sitting there. I had been so focused on getting to Samuel and Grant that I failed to see the car parked on the road.

"You got a new car?"

"I got a raise, baby," Samuel says as he gets into his car. He gives me a mock salute before driving into the street and away from view.

Standing here until his car disappears, I look down at the brown manila envelope in my hands that holds an offer I don't care about.

⤺

"A friend from the city?"

I wasn't expecting him to say a single word to me given how he reacted last night, but I suppose everyone finding out losing the horse funding has sort of made everything else irrelevant.

A 'hi' or a 'good morning' would have been a pleasant way to start the day, but I assume Grant spent all of last night thinking about Samuel. Samuel was nice enough to let me know that he's spoken to a couple of people, and they would be reaching out to me soon.

He also mentioned that Greg Sr. is expecting to hear from me, and it would be good if I'm able to speak to him soon before he drives down to find me. I guess I'm flattered that my absence is causing so much disruption in the company. Maybe they did actually value me. It makes me happy to know that in my absence, things weren't running smoothly. It's the ego boost I needed to keep going through my day.

"We worked for the same company," I reply because until Samuel showed up at Willow Falls, I didn't consider him a friend. He was just a coworker, and maybe shared a common dislike for our boss.

"What did he want?"

I already know that Grant knows exactly what Samuel wanted, but if he's going to play dumb, then I'm going to give him the grace he needs to see it through.

"The company wants me back."

Grant grunts in reply, and I find myself waiting for him to say something. He fixes his eyes on the horse in front of him, watching her eat the hay from the pile in front of her.

No one knows what the plan is with these horses, but until my father is ready to decide, they're going to keep taking care of them. Sooner or later, they'll have to get rid of them to make space for the new ones who are going to take their place.

"Are you going to take the offer?"

I let out the breath I must have been holding in this entire time. The last conversation like this spiraled into disagreement and a fight. A repeat is the last thing we need, but what's the right move in a situation like this?

"I don't know, Grant. I really don't know. They're offering me an apartment upgrade, good and flexible work hours, and extended vacation time. I'm going to be head of a department and train new architects for the company. I'm going to be something close to a board member. I don't know what happened that's making them try their hardest to cling to me like this, but I'm terrified of what will happen if I don't take advantage of it."

Grant grunts again, and I resist the urge to pull my hair. I want him to say more instead of grunting like I'm saying something in passing. Even though we haven't gotten there yet, this possible flirting we've been doing has started to mean something to me. Not that he is the highlight of my day, but I've started to look forward to these little interactions.

"I'm not trying to run away from you," I say as I reach for his hand. "I admit the way I handled things as a kid was less than appealing, but can you trust that I know what I'm doing now?"

Grant turns away from the horse to look at me. "Are you asking me to trust you to make decisions for us or for you?"

I bite my lip because it doesn't sound okay hearing it from him.

"I don't know what I want. I don't know if I want to stay in Willow Falls or if I want to return to the city and get my job back. Or a different one for that matter. These questions constantly keep me up at night. I came here to relax. I just need time to figure it out. I'm not even sure what is going on with us."

Grant nods his head. "I understand that, and the last thing I want is for you to feel overwhelmed by all of this. We haven't seen each other for a long time, and I guess I still carry that hurt with me. I'm not going to ask you to put your life on hold because of this thing I've been feeling rekindled between us. But I still feel something for you, Alexis, and I hope you don't ditch me and just up and leave like you did the last time. I hope you talk to me so we can figure something out that we both have input in.

If moving to the city is going to work for you, we can figure things out. I can visit the city, and if the city gets too much for you, I'll be here waiting for you in Willow Falls. As your friend or whatever you decide. I won't hate you for picking yourself over everything else. I could never hate you. Trust me, I've tried and had a lot of time to master it, but it's not something I can feel for you. So, Wildflower, do whatever works for you. I think I'm old enough to understand it now. Whatever you need, however you need it, I'm here for you. Just let me in this time, and be there for you."

The nickname warms my heart and I smile softly, ignoring the burn in my eyes. Maybe talking about things works. I really should've just talked to him instead of just making decisions by myself. It wasn't always just about me.

Grant's expression is soft, and I move closer to him to wrap my arms around him. He hugs me back, pressing my body closer to his. We stay like that for a while, basking in each other's warmth, and I can't help wondering if we're going to be alright.

Maybe not immediately, but somehow, someway, things have shifted between us, and the future doesn't feel so scary.

Chapter Eighteen

The wildflower field is empty, and I'm sitting underneath the large oak with my eyes closed. I'm taking a break after a long morning of pulling weeds on the farm. My mother had told me it was alright if I didn't work with the farmhands, but Grant was working and I was subtly trying to spend a lot of time with him.

It's clingy, I know, but Grant has yet to call me out on it, and if he doesn't say anything, I don't get why I have to be the one to bring it up. It's guilt that fuels me and the desire to do something right by him because he has done nothing but be understanding of me.

Going back to the city and to keep working under conditions dictated by me is not an opportunity that a lot of people are going to get; I'm not crazy enough to not realize that.

The thing about my line of work is, even though I'm well-seasoned, someone younger and better, with fresher ideas, is always out there waiting to be discovered, waiting for just the right person to vouch for them.

There's still the question of whether or not I would like to remain in Willow Falls. When I decided to up and leave with little plan, part of that plan was to call my building manager and ask her to oversee the moving of my things.

I wonder what it means that I never got around to that. That if I decided to up and leave right this moment, there would still be a roof over my head in the city. The wheels in my head are spinning when I feel someone settle beside me.

Grant looks at me with a smile on his face. "I saw you from a distance and wanted to say hello."

I relax my shoulders, letting them sag a little, and my weight leans a little to the side into Grant; it's nobody's business, especially not when Grant adjusts a little to accommodate me.

"Thinking about the horses?"

The horses are the last thing on my mind at the moment, but he's offering an easy out, so I decide to follow the white lie. My actual thoughts are too consuming and confusing.

"I can't believe we're about to lose all of them."

"Your father made a decision?" Grant asks, and I remember my father talking to him after we got back from the meeting, no doubt telling him what had transpired. Since then, both my parents have worn forlorn looks, and I knew it wasn't just about the money. Those horses mean a lot to them. They mean a lot to all of us.

"I mean, not all of them. Just the older ones."

"Like Aster."

Grant turns his head to look at me. "They're not going to kill her; you know that, right? Your father wouldn't let that happen. He's just going to move them to a local stable, and maybe Aster would be lucky to find a youngin' to care for her, like you once did with Daisy. Then there's Primrose, she's going to be in a pageant or something."

I remember Primrose. I'm not fond of that particular horse, but I've seen Rose, her nickname, in action and she's our next best runner beside Aster. Making her do pageants rub me in some bad way.

"No breeding for her?"

"Don't even play about that. The plan might include making Rose and Sorrel have a kid together. That foal will sell for possibly millions. Rose and Sorrel are fine specimens, they just happen to be too old to participate in the race for the county."

Sorrel is an Arabian stallion and runs like *the Flash*. His mother was bred with the best thoroughbred in town.

I seem to be the only one who's taking this too hard, as my parents appear to be making plans to swap the horses. Last night, I overheard them talking about it in my father's office, and I had tried listening, but they are very good at talking in hushed tones.

A part of me wishes they'd just let me help—or at the very least include me in the conversations. Phone books sit open across the table, pages flipped to names I've never even heard before. The only thing that's clear is that my parents are determined to get their hands on some horses.

I wonder if I'll be able to find someone who can get them good horses. If I ask Samuel about it, would he be able to make some calls and find a good seller? What if I add it as one of the clauses for why I'd take the job I'm being offered? Would Greg Sr. do everything to make sure that my conditions are met?

"My parents aren't telling me anything. They keep saying that it's nothing to worry about, and it makes me feel like I'm not here in Willow Falls, like I'm calling on the phone and they're trying to delude me into thinking things are fine."

Grant lets out a thoughtful "*huh*", shuffling a bit so he can wrap an arm around me. I give up the pretense and relax further into him. His body heat warms me up even though I'm not cold. His cologne smells of wood and mandarin today. Manly and sweet at the same time. I'm happy that I get the chance to have this moment with him.

"It's because things are fine. There's no need for them to make you worry if things are really fine."

"Do you know that for sure?"

Grant nods his head. "Yes. If it weren't fine, lying to you would be a waste of time because, one way or another, you're going to find out. I think what you should be concerned about is the fest coming up."

I look at him with confusion. "Why should I be concerned about the festival?"

"I know it's been a while, but Alexis, this is an important event for all of us. It's probably one of the only events that focuses on the folks of Willow Falls. This helps bring in money for the town so we can continue to do the things we do. Everyone is expected to get on board with it. Everyone, including you, Wildflower."

I furrow my brows, ignoring the way my cheeks burn again at the nickname. "That's not what the flyer says. I hear there's a call for volunteers."

"That's just something for the tourists who will still be around during that time. The rest of us have a mandated duty to show up."

"So, you'll be showing up to help then?"

"The structures aren't going to put themselves up."

I press my lips together and try not to go through my mental collection of Grant doing hard labor. Of him with his shirt sleeves rolled up or no shirt at all, his veins on full display and muscles taut as he pushes a wheelbarrow full of dirty straw and debris up and down the farm.

The idea that this image is going to be on full display for the whole town to gawk at unsettles something in me. I know I'm being ridiculous as I burrow myself further into him, but I can't help it.

In a way Grant has always been mine. I just never realized it until now.

Chapter Nineteen

"**Y**our mother says you've been getting along *very* well with Grant."

Josie takes a sip of her lemonade, maintaining eye contact with me.

"When have I not gotten along with him? And why do you keep gossiping about me with my mother?"

"Gossiping?" Josie asks, placing one hand on her chest while daring to look offended by the idea that I think she gossips about me for that matter. "She was merely informing me of all the things I'm missing out on since I don't live here with you. The last time we talked, you didn't know how you felt about Grant or if you're willing to settle down in Willow Falls."

Looking away, my eyes find the barn. We're sitting on the porch, watching the movers try to haul Primrose and Aster into their trailer so they can take them to their new home. From up here, I can see Grant trying to help.

He's not the only farmhand lending assistance, but he's the only one my eyes zero in on. He moves with the confidence of a thousand people, hanging onto the lead fastened around Aster.

Aster is unwilling to be moved, and her reactions are unsettling Primrose. Rose keeps trying to get away, but the farmhand holding her lead knows how to keep her calm. He's patting her mane and trying to distract her from Aster, who keeps acting like she's being led to a slaughterhouse.

"I've thought about it a lot," I say, still looking out at the barn. "Do I want to give up my career for a man?"

Josie makes a startling noise at the back of her throat. "What are you talking about giving up your career for him? Is that how you've been looking at it?"

Confused, I look back at Josie. "What do you mean?"

"Alexis, coming to Willow Falls is something you decided on because you couldn't take what was being dished out to you there. You came back to take a break, and you had no idea what the break was going to look like. Grant was not a factor in your returning to Willow Falls. You had no idea he was even here. I'm not saying that you shouldn't consider him now, I'm saying that you should look at it objectively.

Are you well rested? If you go back to that environment, how are you going to respond to it? Does the thought of going back to work, the same work you left, working for the same person and with the same people, fill you with excitement or dread? Does the salary offer any compensation? Does it fuel you with the drive to endure it? When you do endure it, have you decided how long you're going to endure it for? Or is it for the rest of your life? Are you going to regret coming back to Willow Falls and seeing Grant with someone else? What about life in the city? Will you feel complete going back to the city?"

But Josie doesn't stop there. "If you can answer all of this honestly, then I assure you that things are going to work out for you. You're not the only one who has had to leave the big city and all of its promises to come back to Willow Falls.

Although our circumstances are a lot different, I also left to save myself. I know we haven't talked about it much because we're both busy, but I used to date this guy in the city. He was a walking daydream, perfect on paper. And I thought that I'd seen someone who could support me in everything I was doing because all the men I've dated are complete trash."

I'm a trash friend.

"But as perfect as he was, as shiny as the relationship was on paper, he was an asshole in reality. When all you want for yourself are just ideas, nearly everyone will claim to support it. But when it starts to take shape, then you know who really wants to fly with you. He didn't want me to even walk, let alone fly.

Willow Falls not only heals you; it gives you room to have everything you dreamed of. Just because it worked out like that for me doesn't mean it'll do that for you. You need to figure out what it is you want and how you're going to go about it. Grant's not the main point of focus; he's just a contributing factor. Have you even thought about placing your career somewhere else?"

My mouth is dry as I watch my friend narrate my ordeal with the most serious face I've ever seen on her. The knowledge that Josie, who's full of life, had gone through something as awful as dating an asshole makes me want to sob on behalf of my friend. Especially since I couldn't be there for her.

It makes me regret my choice of cutting people off because it's becoming more obvious that it was a selfish decision on my part. It's clear to me now that all the people I cut off were people that were—and still are—dear to my heart, and all these people would have needed someone to talk to, and I just wasn't there for them.

Now they're here for me, trying to comfort me, giving me advice, and making sacrifices for me to make sense of my life, and I don't know what to do about it.

"I'm sorry you had to go through that," is all I can offer now.

Josie smiles at me, but the smile doesn't quite reach her eyes. "It's alright. I needed something to build my character after all. Plus it led me back here."

"I think your character is great, always has been. I'm glad you were able to get through that and you had the right support to get through it. It makes me realize that maybe my issues are not as serious as I'm making them out to be."

"That's not why I told you my story, though," Josie says and sets her glass of lemonade on the table. "You used to be so smart; did all the fumes get to you out there?"

I laugh at that because as kids we loved the smell of gasoline. But all those years, those smells in the city, they aren't so pleasant.

"What I'm saying is, you should focus on what's going to bring you the greatest satisfaction. Whether it's staying here in Willow Falls to see what can potentially become of you and Grant or, going back to the city to see what your career can become if you go after it with all you have. You need to be able to look back and realize that you did all of that and feel absolutely no regrets. This is your one life, and if you let it go because you made some decisions in the past that you're trying to rectify, you're going to lose yourself. Leave the past in the past and create a new future. You can still have a career in Willow Falls.

If I know anything about Grant, it's that he wouldn't want you to throw your life away because of him. As long as you talk to him, maintain a clear communication network with him, things will be fine. Really, if you do choose to go away, please talk to the man. I don't want a repeat of what happened in the past. I nearly lost my mind trying to get him to calm down because you broke up with him out of the blue."

My heart is immediately crushed all over again hearing Josie tell me how much I hurt Grant.

"Don't do that to him again. Don't do that to me again. We're friends first and foremost, and that should matter more than anything else. I want you in my life, and I'd hope you want me in your life. That means through the good and the bad. When things get hard, I'd like to be there for you. So please don't cut me off. Don't cut any of us off this time. That makes people worry, and I worried a lot because of you. So, for the love of God, whatever you decide, bring us along. We love you more than anything."

Tears well up in my eyes, and I have to look away to stop them from falling. I laugh a little, hoping the tears will stay exactly where they are and, if possible, dissipate.

I look back to the barn, and it seems like they've managed to put the horses into the trailers. Aster is no longer neighing like her life depends on it, assuming she's accepted her fate of leaving us. I planned to be there to say goodbye, but watching from a distance made more sense to me.

I can't afford to start crying, not that staying away from the scene is changing anything since Josie has decided to tug at my heartstrings.

My mother clings to my father as they watch the truck disappear down the drive. The weight of it all is written plainly across both of their faces, and not for the first time, it strikes me how lucky they are to have each other. Someday, I hope to share something like that with someone too.

My eyes wander to the left and I find Grant. He's standing with his farm hat clutched to his chest like a prayer is being offered for the safety of the horses. His tanned skin, from hours and hours of outside work, seems to glow under the setting sun, and I let myself drink it in.

I could stay for the life it seems we'd have here, but there's a part of me that wonders what life might look like on my own terms, where the job doesn't drain me or leave me feeling like the air's been pulled from my lungs.

A job that will provide me with the security that I need. And I think for the first time, why I can't have both Grant and a steady job. The thought startles me out of my head to find Grant looking in my direction.

It's unclear if he can see me, but I turn my head to look at Josie, who's already looking at me. The glass of lemonade is back in her hand, and she's now cleaning the droplets of water off the cup with the tissue resting on the table.

"I hope you both know how gone you are for each other. Not to be the one to bring it to your attention, but you could be something if you're both willing to put in the work. By that, I mean don't run off again. Do you see the way he looks at you, Lex? You need Willow Falls, and it needs you."

I blush at the accusation and turn my head back towards Grant. He's no longer looking my way, now talking to my father. But from this distance, it's easy to make out my mother's face, and I can tell that she has a small smile on her face.

What could they be talking about?

Chapter Twenty

"**I**'m going to take the job," I tell my parents over dinner. I'm looking down at my plate of mashed potatoes, waiting for their reactions. When neither of them say anything immediately, I'm forced to lift my head up to look at them.

My parents exchange a look, and my heart hammers in my chest. There's no telling how they'll react to my news, so I hold my breath while waiting, hoping for a positive response.

When they look back at me, my mother is unable to hide the skepticism in her voice. "That's it? You're just deciding like that?"

"Yeah, I figured that I've spent enough time here, and I'm feeling refreshed. It makes sense to go back to work, right? With some of the horses gone, that's less for you both to worry about, especially with the help from Grant. The longer I stay here, the harder it'll be to find a job. And I need a job."

My father nods his head. "Okay, um... that's good. If that's what you want, sweetie. If you're sure you feel relaxed and if you're ready to take on your job, we're in full support of your decision, you know that we'll always support you. We just hope this is really what you want."

His smile is genuine and when I look back to my mom, the same look is reflected on her face. My shoulders relax, and I realize just how tense I was waiting for their response.

I have yet to send out a reply to the job offer. The hope is to walk into Foster's with a signed copy of the offer, and a smile. The way everything has unfolded still feels unreal. What are the odds that all of this happened to me just because I quit my job in the first place?

"When are you set to return to the city then?" my father asks, the smile still on his face.

"I figured Monday would be my first day back," I say slowly and wait for my parents to remember what day it is today and do the math from there.

It's Saturday today, which means that Monday is the day after tomorrow. I see the exact moment the days dawn on my mother.

"You can't be serious," my mother says, standing up, throwing her napkin. "You're going to get up and leave like that? Why not stay another week? This is all so sudden."

"I've been out of a job for a while now. I don't want to be out of practice, Mom. I should take advantage of their offer while it's there. I'm scared that if I keep putting it off, they're going to take away the offer. All the jobs I've been applying for haven't gotten back to me, and I'd like to take advantage of this one now. So, I leave tomorrow. I will be able to get to my apartment by evening and get ready for work on Monday. I already texted Samuel."

My explanation makes a lot of sense, and I can tell that my parents see it too. My father isn't going to argue; I've known the man my whole life, he's a supporter through and through. A cheerleader in his own right, if you decide on something, he's going to offer advice and then cheer you on whether you decide to do what his advice is or not.

This left all the resistance up to my mother. My mother always had to ask a lot of questions. Like she's currently doing right now.

"How about you go back in three weeks? It won't be too late, right? The festival is in three weekends, Alexis. You should at least stay for that. Can't you just ask them for an extension or tell them when you'll start?"

"I want to stay for that too, Mom," I tell her, remembering all the plans I made with Grant to volunteer for the preparations. It's supposed to be a nice night together, but now I'm going to have to let it all go because I want to see what my life can be like if I go back to the city. This fresh mindset, my friends back, and a goal for my future.

"Then stay. What will it hurt?"

"The job, Mom. I've already told you it's important. I want you to understand that I'm trying to do something for myself here and also helping the farm, and this means me going back to the city and returning to work. I can come back every last weekend of the month if this is about me not returning for the last decade. I can be here every other week. You just don't need me here everyday, and I need to get back to a job."

My mother purses her lips and I know that I've hit the nail on the head. She's reluctant to let me go because she fears I won't come back.

Maybe the list of people I've hurt exceeds my friends. I've fucked up more than I ever knew, and I know that given the chance, I'd like to make it all right. Communicate properly with my parents and friends. Maintain contact with them and share my burdens with them.

Which is why I'm telling them the real reason why I have to go back.

"You didn't call the last time you left." This time it's my father that speaks, and somehow that's worse for me. "You also didn't take our calls when we called. We worry about you, Alexis. You're all we have."

I look down and nod my head, not bothering to hold back my tears. How do I reassure them that it's going to be different this time? Even if I say it, they're not going to believe it. I have to show them.

"I promise you," I say, reaching forward to hold their hand in each of mine. "I promise that it's going to be different this time. I'm going to call every day or, at the very least, three times a week. If you call, I'm going to answer. But if I'm in a position where I can't answer immediately, I'm going to send a text to acknowledge the call, and then I'll call when I can. I promise to not shut you out this time." *Please believe me.*

My sincerity wins in the end because my mother nods her head and places a kiss at the back of my hand. "That's all we want. And I hope you were smart enough to make the same promises to Grant."

⚘

It's automatic now to go find Grant at the wildflower field. I'm not sure he'll be there tonight, but I hope he will. There's no guarantee that I'll see him before I leave, if I don't manage to tonight.

I'm leaving first thing tomorrow to beat the morning traffic. I don't want to say this to him on the phone because if there's one thing being at Willow Falls has taught me, it's that communication is going to solve a lot of my issues. And when I leave Willow Falls, I hope to still be in communication with both Grant and Josie.

The night wind blows past me and ruffles my hair. I reach out and try to tame it down, but it's a useless effort. I should have worn my hat, but I was more focused on getting to the field when I saw a shadow move in that direction from my window.

Now, the closer I get, the more I wonder if my eyes are seeing things. Did I really see someone—Grant—go in that direction? Or was my mind simply playing tricks on me? The lights are still on by the barn, which means someone is still out here.

Honestly, if I don't see him tonight, my backup plan is to stop at the garage on my way out of town and hope that he's there so I can tell him goodbye. Somehow, this time, it feels paramount that I say goodbye to him face-to-face, just like I had done to Josie earlier today.

She was sad to hear that I would be leaving town when I just got back, but I promised to visit a lot, and that's a promise that I'm going to keep.

When I finally reach the field, Grant is nowhere to be found. My shoulders fall, and I let out a sigh. This isn't going well for me. I hoped to spend one last night with him, hold him, and tell him how much I'm going to miss him.

The wildflowers sway with the light wind, and I forcefully shove my hair out of the way, a little rougher than I did earlier. I rub my face and resist the urge to stomp my foot like a child who didn't get her way.

"Looking for me?" The voice startles me, and when I whip my head in the direction of the voice, I find Grant sitting underneath the tree we call our spot. I swore that I looked in that direction, but now that he's there looking like he hadn't been anywhere else, I'm wondering if I even looked.

A smile spreads across my face as I hurry toward him, abandoning any pretense that he isn't the exact person I came to the field to see. He stands as I get closer, and I lean in to hug him.

"Do you have time to sit?" Grant says.

"Yes."

I settle next to him and turn to him with a smile.

The light from the lamppost in the corner of the field pours down and lights up Grant's skin in a way that makes it look golden. I'm positive that I won't find anyone as lovely as him in this lifetime. And probably the next.

"You seem excited," Grant says, and I visibly deflate because the reason I'm here is nothing pleasant. I don't know how Grant is going to take the news, and there's no way to tell if he's going to be excited for me, even though he's claimed over and over that he's going to be in support of whatever decision I decide to take in the end.

"I wasn't sure if I'd be able to see you tonight," I confess as Grant lifts his hand to tuck a loose strand of my hair behind my ear.

"Well, you'd have seen me tomorrow anyway," Grant says, and my shoulders sink further. Grant catches it and raises a brow. "Is something wrong?"

"I've decided to take the job offer," I say, looking everywhere but at the man in front of me. When Grant doesn't reply immediately, I'm forced to look his way. His gaze is on me, and his lips are slightly parted.

My heart hammers in my chest as I wait for him to process the news and say something.

"That's—" Grant starts, but the sentence is never completed. He clears his throat and sits up straighter. "When are you leaving?"

I look away again and tuck more strands of my hair behind my ear. I clear my throat, unsure now if deciding to leave tomorrow is a good idea. But the truth is, I'm scared that if I don't take this offer, a better one will never come along. And if another one doesn't come along, what is going to become of this career I've painstakingly tried to build? I put my all into being an architect.

And what if another one does come and I never manage to get as far as I am now? Is that something I'll be okay with? Can I truthfully look back on my life and not regret not taking the offer? Ugh, why can't this be a simple decision to make?

The truth is that I have no idea. I know I'll regret it if I reject this job and things don't pan out the way I want. That's why I'm taking the offer, that's why I'm going back to the city and try to make something better out of this chance I've been given.

"I leave tomorrow."

"Tomorrow? That's too soon."

"I know, but I'm running out of time, and I don't want to stay here and miss the chance I've been given. I didn't want to leave this time without letting you know. I don't want a repeat of what happened the last time."

Grant doesn't say anything, and I ready myself for whatever he may say because at the end of the day, I do deserve his wrath. I might be leaving with every intention to keep in touch with him, but that doesn't mean that I'm not taking him by surprise with the news.

"I appreciate that, but damn, I wish I had a little warning. Don't get me wrong, I knew you were going to take the offer, I just assumed I'd be given a little time to prepare for it. If you know what I mean."

His meaning is clear, so I just nod. No words come in my defense; silence remains while waiting for him to decide the way forward for both of us.

"I'm going to miss you so much," Grant says finally and reaches for my hand. He pulls me to him and wraps his arms around me. I rest my head on his chest and wrap my arms around him.

This went a lot easier than I thought it would. A part of me had imagined a lot of yelling, but Grant had always been the most understanding of the two of us. Not for the first time either, but I feel incredibly lucky to be given a second chance at this. With him. Even if it ends up with us just staying friends.

"I'm going to call you every day until you get sick of me and block my number."

Grant laughs like it's the funniest thing he's ever heard. "I don't think I can ever get sick of you, Lex."

He tightens his arms around me, and I don't move away from him. I settle into the embrace and allow both of us this time together because it's going to be a little while before we can do it again.

"I can come visit you in the city," he says as he lays a gentle kiss on the top of my head.

I love the sound of that. I tighten my arms around him and bury my face in his chest, inhaling his cologne.

"I'd really love that," I say.

Feeling Grant relax, I smile again. We're going to be alright.

Chapter Twenty-One

Monday morning finds me sitting in my car in front of Foster's Architect. My heart is hammering, and it's the same old dread that I felt before. Only this time, the reason for it is different. Did I make the right choice coming back here? That last night with Grant was all I needed. But here we are.

It feels like my first day at work ever, but the excitement of being in a new environment and meeting new people is absent. I know the two Gregs will be present because Samuel was kind enough to let me know that he informed them I'll be rejoining the company today.

And Greg Sr. decided that he'll need to be there to thank me for honoring his invitation to come back to him so they could take the company to even greater heights.

My fear, I realized mid-deep breath, is stemming from the fact that I don't know how to be around these people anymore. Without a doubt, they're going to respect me because how many people can say they got invited to rejoin a company after they quit? Add to that all the added benefits? How many people can say they're so good at their job that the founder of the company they worked for personally wrote their new offer and was waiting inside to welcome them back in, even though they've long retired?

Nearly nobody, because the chances of that happening are actually next to none. I just so happened to be the one in a million.

I step out of the car in one of my many black suits. My closet is still untouched and I realize for the first time that all the outfits I have are of the monochrome variety. A shade of black and white. Nothing colorful, unlike what I was wearing in Willow Falls.

"Ms. Larson," the receptionist greets with a bright smile, "it's so nice to have you back with us."

I just smile, mostly because I'm sure that if I open my mouth to talk, my voice will quake. The point of wearing this particular black suit is to give the air of control. This is my power suit, the one I put on when I want to show that I'm not taking any nonsense.

There isn't any distracting pattern on the suit, and it doesn't cling to me in a manner that might be perceived as seductive. It's a wide-leg suit and barely form-fitting.

It makes me feel whole and secure, like armor. It's one of my favorite pieces, and I made sure to go to an Italian tailor for it.

I take the elevator, the smile still on my face as the door slides closed. The second it starts moving, I lose my smile, grateful that they didn't opt for one of those see through elevators regardless of how many times it came up in a meeting.

Another deep breath, and I shake my body a little; an attempt to get rid of all the pent-up feelings. *I can do this.* This being something I've done nearly half my life.

It's like I took a vacation and I'm coming back to work after. Surely everyone would make a big deal out of it like that one time Greg Jr. went on vacation and they had to bake a cake and hang balloons in order to give him what Samuel described as the perfect welcome-back-to-work gift.

Eyeroll.

I close my eyes and take one last deep breath, enough to get me through what's waiting for me once the elevator slides open and then the rest of the day. I repeat mantras over and over in my head, willing myself to believe that I'm deserving of this opportunity, telling myself that whatever happens, I'm going to give my best and not let a repeat of what happened before happen again.

This is my life, and I'm going to make the best of it.

The elevator comes to a stop, and the door slides open. I open my eyes and step out of the elevator. A loud pop greets me, and confetti falls on my head. There's a round of clapping and Greg Sr. is standing in front of me with outstretched arms.

I shake his hand, barely aware of what he's saying. Once he lets go of my hand, Greg Jr. is in front of me, a grin on his face as he shakes my hand up and down. He says something, but all of it is drowned by the incessant clapping and whistling, and I feel like I've just come back from sealing the deal to be the architect of the White House or something.

I want to rub my head but manage to stop myself, ignoring the way my head is starting to hurt and the tiredness that is creeping up my spine. How is this my life?

All the noise is overwhelming to me, and one would think I've been away from the city for nearly twenty years with the way that every sudden sound seems like it's going to push me into the deep end.

Greg Jr. moves to the side, a grin still present on his face, and then Samuel is in front of me with cake in his hands. He's smiling at me, and I know that if he had one hand free, he'd throw me a thumbs-up.

Samuel has made it known that what I'm doing, what I have managed to achieve—getting invited back to work in this manner—is next to winning a presidential election with no campaign whatsoever.

I don't quite feel like I've won anything, but I stay put, shaking hands here and there. Accepting every 'welcome back' thrown my way until I start to consider that the only reason that many people are excited to see me back is the break everyone is taking and the free cake.

It's red velvet. I hate red velvet.

We continue for a few moments until it becomes obvious to everyone that they're putting off their work, and the continuous merriment is starting to seem ridiculous. More welcomes are thrown my way, and finally, I find myself in Greg Sr.'s office.

There are four of us in this office: the two Gregs, me, and Samuel. I take one of the visitors' seats with Samuel by my side. Greg Sr. sits in the main chair, a seat that would have been otherwise reserved for his son.

Greg Jr. stands by his father's side with his arm resting on the headrest. From where I'm seated, he looks like an exotic bird on display, and I wonder if he knows that.

There's a smile on his face as he regards me, like I'm back by his efforts and not by that of his father. I almost want to beg the older man to come back from retirement. For some reason, I feel like I'd be able to handle working for him rather than his son.

But then again, Greg Jr. must be on strict instructions to make sure that I don't leave again. I'm determined to make the most of being back. I'm going to lead this company to even more success and make leaving Willow Falls this time worth the distance.

"I'm so glad you decided to come back," Greg Sr. says. "I hope the rest you had did you a lot of good."

I smile at him. "I'm glad you thought I was worth all of the stress. It makes me happy that my contributions to the company meant something to all of you."

Greg Sr. waves his hand in the air, as if he's hoping to wave my words away. "I will never underestimate the role you play here. You took me by surprise because my son and I were convinced that you really loved it here. We're a family, and I would like for us to communicate better. Okay?"

I nod my head automatically, smart enough to know when I'm being scolded.

Greg Sr. smiles one last time in my direction before getting to his feet. "I'm going to leave you all to it. I'm hoping for good results."

Now, everyone is standing as Sr. walks out of the room, accompanied by his son, even after he insisted on being able to walk himself out. Sometimes, I find it hard to tell if Greg Jr. really adores his father or if he just wants to appear that way.

I've been treated a few times of tales about his father. Some I knew, and others took me by surprise because no one should be giving out that much information about their family.

"I can't believe you came back," Samuel says when both Gregs step out of the room.

"Well, I figured this is as good as it gets, and turning down an offer like this, in hopes it wasn't the wrong decision, didn't sit well with me."

"And your man back home? How did he take it?"

I slide my eyes to Samuel and he raises his hand in surrender.

"I have eyes. He was glaring at me the entire time I was there, like I was the bearer of bad news. Don't expect me to think he took you moving back well."

I smile coyly because I see it for the first time through someone else's eyes. Just how considerate Grant is of me. "Well, since you asked, he did take it well. We plan to stay in touch better, and I'll be taking my vacation days as promised."

Samuel whistles. "Good for you. On another note, there's a lot for you to tackle. There's going to be a meeting today with the board where you'll meet and hear the proposal for the team you'll be leading. You'll then look over the document sent over by the new clients we're hoping to take on. It's an international project, but not somewhere too far. The location hasn't been decided, but it's a restaurant this time. They need it in four locations, each one holding the essence of the organization while leaning into the culture of the new locations. They're thinking Japan, Australia, maybe even Spain."

I whistle.

Samuel nods his head. "I'll bring over the file to you after this. You have your work cut out for you. And I'm saying this to you because I feel like we've built a rapport, but don't really pay attention to all the goodies they're offering you. You're on probation and expected not to slack off."

I stop short. "What?"

"You left abruptly; we lost a client. It was a whole thing. Nobody's happy, but if you're here we can score more clients, earn more money. Your reputation precedes you, and some clients show up looking for you. Word of mouth or whatever, but you hurt the company. So don't relax just yet if you intend to stay here."

"Why would you tell me this now? And why was this not in the contract? Are you going to get in trouble for letting me know?"

Samuel scoffs, like the idea of him getting in trouble here is laughable. "I'm loyal to the company, but we started off together. If I thought telling you this would somehow come back to bite me in the neck, I wouldn't have bothered. Besides, what would they do without me? Oh, by the way, you have a new email since your last one expired."

Later, when I run the conversation over in my head, I realize how right Samuel had been; what would Greg Jr. do without him? He's set to retire with the man if all goes right. Greg Jr. is so sneaky, I wouldn't put it past him to threaten Samuel into staying.

I just need to focus on making this work for me.

Chapter Twenty-Two

Two weeks after being back in the city, it occurs to me that something is incredibly wrong, and while this is a type of realization that can happen to anyone, it's not something that should happen to me while I'm in the middle of a meeting two hours in and I have no idea what's going on.

I blink back into the room slowly and try to sit up without calling too much attention to myself. There's a notepad in front of me, and there's nothing there except Grant's name in various cursive fonts and a few poorly scribbled flowers.

I flush and turn the page, hoping nobody else saw that I've been scribbling a man's name on my notepad while they were discussing the future of the company. The only thing I did hear is that the team I'm supposed to be overseeing is taking off sometime next month.

I make a mental note to ask for an assistant to take note of these things in the case I miss them. My lack of attention might be stemming from the fact that I'm doing a lot of late-night calls with Grant. Or that I'm in the office from five in the morning until seven at night most days.

Every night I've spent away from Willow Falls has ended with me giving a breakdown of my day to Grant, keeping him looped in while he does the same. I know that the town's fest is coming along really well, and my mother's ankle doesn't hurt quite as much.

She's still going to be resting a lot, and my father is also not exerting himself, which means all the requirements and tasks for running the farm have fallen to Grant, who always says he's more than happy to be of assistance.

"And that concludes the meeting for today," Greg Jr. announces, pulling me back into the room. Everyone is starting to gather their things, and I try to maintain a passive expression, as if I'm aware of everything that has been going on. "If you have any questions or any ideas, be sure to run them through Ms. Larson. I'm certain she'll need all the support she can get to see that this project is a success."

Glad to be mentally present in the room while this is said, I force a smile on my face and look at the faces of all my colleagues. Some smile back at me and give me a thumbs up, a couple nod their heads but don't look in my direction. Then there are those that don't bother looking at me but make sure to roll their eyes.

I would roll my eyes, too, if I weren't the object of the discourse.

One by one, everyone files out of the room, but I remain seated and amongst the last people to leave the room. Greg Jr. takes my being seated as an opportunity to talk to me. Samuel stands loyally by his side.

"I know coming back and experiencing all of this can be a little overwhelming," he says, and I have to fight the urge to squint my eyes at him. He does look a little sincere, and I'm wondering how he became so insightful. "If there's anything we can do to help you ease back into the company and assist in this project, be sure to let us know. We are, after all, one family."

I nod my head. "Of course, I'll do just that."

Greg Jr. walks out of the conference room with Samuel hot on his tail, rattling off everything on his schedule with practiced ease. I let out the breath I didn't even know I was holding, hoping that the day would end already.

A few hours later, a knock sounds on my office door, and I lift my head to find Samuel pushing the door open. Behind him is a man I've never seen before. I thank the heavens first for the break they've granted me because since I opened the document in front of me, I haven't been able to register even a single word.

"Ms. Larson, this is Edward Smith, your new assistant," Samuel states, gesturing at the man standing beside him with a smile on his face.

I raise a brow and move my eyes from Samuel to the man who's wearing a suit jacket that is bigger than him, denim pants, and a tie that looks like it belongs in the sixties. He's all smiles, looking like this is the best thing that could happen to him, and I suppose it is.

Getting a job in this company, regardless of the position, is something that will only be a dream for most people. When I got the job, I remembered being unable to believe it. Three months in, I was constantly waiting for someone to come up to me and tell me there was a mistake and I had to go. Foster's Architect is one of the most prestigious companies to work for in this city.

"My new assistant? I don't get to interview one myself?"

Samuel shrugs his shoulders, and that's all I need to know that I don't exactly have a choice in the matter. "The boss decided that you must need one right away, given all the tasks that you have to take on now. Someone to make sure that you don't get overwhelmed. And Edward here is one of our best guys. If it's any consolation, I personally trained him."

It's a consolation, but that's beside the point. There's something to be said for all the initiative they're taking to make sure I'm comfortable.

"Do you have qualifications?"

"Architecture," Edward says, his voice airy like he's high on something other than the feeling of being there.

"You studied architecture? Why are you playing assistant?"

Edward looks over to Samuel for assistance as if he doesn't know the reason why, either.

"He's shadowing you and taking note of what you do while on the job. Think of him as a mini you, if he knows everything you know, you won't have to worry about anything going off the rails while you're absent."

Samuel maintains eye contact when he says this, and I don't have to be fluent in the language to understand the handwriting on the wall. First, I'm on probation and then next, they're inviting someone in under the guise of being my assistant.

It's laughable that they're asking me to train my own replacement.

"Well, that's really amazing," I say and get to my feet to shake the hand of the man in front of me. Edward smiles easily, gripping my hand and shaking it aggressively.

"You have no idea how happy I am to be here. I've always admired you and your work. All the designs you've done, I've studied all of them and read all your interviews. I'm truly honored to be here. Thank you so much for agreeing to take a chance on me."

Not sure how to respond, I just plaster a smile on my face. I struggle to pull my hand out of Edward's tight grip before looking at Samuel, who finds the situation incredibly humorous. I wish I could see what he sees, but all I see is an overly eager man who, by no fault of his, has been selected to replace me at the quickest convenience.

It's unbelievable in many ways, and I know I'd be blind to it if Samuel wasn't actively trying to make me see the actual picture here. It's not something I've thought about a lot, but the circumstances remind me of the man I shadowed when I got into the company.

Maybe he didn't just simply move states; the company might have fired him to make me take his spot. The idea makes me shudder.

"I love your enthusiasm, I'm sure we'll get along just great."

It turns out that Edward is incredibly good at what he does. With his help, I'm able to get up-to-date with all of the details surrounding the project I'm going to be leading. I found out they are considering a total of six candidates coming from top universities in the country.

Each candidate will go through three tests to ensure that they are fit to work in the prestigious organization.

That's where I come in. My job isn't only to mentor; I'm also expected to design the tests, give lectures, and assign projects to these young budding architects that the company is going to be calling interns.

These interns are supposed to go from sixty to ten, which means that fifty people are going to be losing their spots. This is worse than the *Hunger Games*, but I suppose it meant something if people knew you were top twenty in a program such as the one we are creating.

The selected ten are going to shadow every architect in the company, learning how to pitch for big businesses, and they will try their hand at leading real-life projects to build their skills. Under supervision, of course.

If I wasn't already in the position I am now, I'd be certain that a program like this was going to catapult me into being one of the finest architects the world has ever known.

The more I read the notes Edward presented me, the more I realize that these interns are going to be getting all the things I wished I had. The company is going to invite world-class architects from different parts of the world to lead them after the initial phase.

They're building the dream team, and the fact that I'm being placed in charge of it, even if it means getting booted later on, will do wonders for my resume. I would laugh if I weren't already exhausted.

"The program is projected to start next month, but that's basically a call to the professors to recommend their best students, or whoever they feel is promising enough to inspire change," Edward tells me, and I nod in understanding.

The man is as promising as Samuel says. But maybe he just possesses that one-mindedness that can come from having someone like Samuel teach you everything you know about assisting someone.

"Is there anything I'm expected to do in that regard?"

Edward nods. "You'll have to come up with the proposal and send it over to be signed by the other head of department, including the boss himself. I can assist with drafting something, and you can look it over and add whatever you'd like."

I nod my head in agreement. "I'd appreciate that."

I know that I don't have the mental capacity to do any thinking of my own. It's best to leave it up to someone who's determined to make a mark. I'll just add whatever I deem relevant. I can get the task done, but with my return I've been swamped with paperwork.

"Do I have any other tasks on my to-do list?"

"For today, none. But tomorrow, you have that meeting with the folks from the restaurant chain."

I take a deep breath and let it out slowly. I completely forgot about that.

Chapter Twenty-Three

"The meeting is nothing serious," Edward tells me as soon as I step into work the next day. I'm starting to think he doesn't go home. It's either that or he has the exact same outfit in large quantities.

I hope it's the former because having enough of the same outfit in the same style and color to last you weeks is completely sad. But I don't want to bring it up because, I have a closet full of the same black suits I'll be replacing soon.

"We're sharing ideas with them today, are we not?"

Edward nods his head. "That's the plan. We'll let them know what we think of their proposal."

I walk into my office and wait until Edward shuts the door behind him. Even though he just became my assistant, it feels like every day Edward knows more about the job than I do.

It's awakening the same old competitive spirit in me, the one that made me neglect myself and health in favor of being up-to-date with everything that was happening with a project. It made me seem aware, placed me as a collaborator for many projects way before my ideas started getting approved.

I don't like it.

"Edward, you need to slow down and take care of yourself sometimes. It's good that you know all of these things, but trust me, you don't want to be the one who's getting all the work with little to no recognition. Don't give them too much to make them feel like they can dump everything on you, but give them enough that they'd think they wouldn't be able to get things done without you."

Edward manages to look sheepish, and I wonder if he understands what I'm saying. Even if it doesn't do much for him, I want to make sure that I'm able to help him understand the importance of not getting taken advantage of.

"I'm sure Samuel must have told you some variety of what I'm talking about, but I'd like to spell it out for you. I left the first time because I felt overwhelmed. There was no work-life balance, and I was doing too much to try and get picked every time because they made it look like they were doing me a favor by picking me. I didn't realize that everyone had relaxed enough that nothing could be done without me being there. I'll pretend not to notice it, but they're trying to replace me with you, and who knows, you might end up being the one leading this project. I don't mind that, I just don't want you to have the same regret I did.

Relax a little; I'll pull my weight too. And today's meeting isn't really about sharing ideas with them. The first meeting is always about listening to whatever they've come up with, going to see the site with them—if it's something we can do—and trying to understand the location and seeing how we can come up with something that can stand out and blend with the environment at the same time."

Edward nods rapidly, and I hope I haven't said so much that will get me in trouble. I hope Edward is not the type of person to go tattling because then I might be out of there sooner than I thought.

"I thought you didn't like me," Edward says with a small smile on his face. Now that he's smiling at me like that, I can see the stark difference between this one and the ones I've been treated to before.

"Why would you think that?"

Edward shrugs. "You never smile at me, and you keep looking like the sound of my voice is irritating to you. I told Samuel about it, I can't believe he never mentioned it to you."

"Samuel and I aren't exactly close, and if he thinks I don't need to know something, he doesn't mention it. I don't dislike you, I've just been distracted a lot lately."

Edward nods his head. "I guess it's because you just came back and there's a lot for you to do. Samuel says that you weren't doing this much initially."

"You're close with Samuel?"

Edward shrugs. "He's nice to me sometimes; other times, he's trying to get me to understand between the lines in a way that makes me want to jump off the building."

I pause, my lips pursed as I take in Edward, looking for signs that the man might need more help than he's letting on. Maybe I should talk to Samuel and get him to let up on him a bit.

"I'm not going to jump off the building," Edward says in a hurry when he catches my expression. "I promise. I overreact sometimes."

"If you say so, but know that if it gets to be too much, you can talk to someone."

"You?"

I shrug my shoulders. "Sure, if that's what you need, but also know we have resources in HR for that as well. While this conversation was nice, I'd like us to keep a clear head when we go into that meeting. And an open mind too because your patience will be tested by their ridiculous demands, and your job is to guide them to see reason and pick a more practical design without making it look like that's what you're doing. But I'm here if you ever need to talk."

"That sounds like a mental workout."

"You haven't the slightest idea."

"Also, I'm done with the proposal," Edward says, and hands it over to me with a sheepish smile on his face.

I accept it with a sigh. "I hope you have friends outside of work."

Edward just laughs.

⚬

"You sound exhausted today," Grant says midway into our conversation, and I realize I'm dozing and coming back into the conversation. I don't remember most of what he's said.

Before Grant called me, I was going through the proposal Edward came up with, and I have to admit that the man has a flair for writing these things. There's not a lot of things to edit, but I have to adjust the tone of a proposal from a suggestion to a request.

I didn't know the difference either until I was taught the right way to write a proposal. I make a mental note to bring it up with Edward. It helps that he's eager to learn.

"I just had a lot to do today. A lot of meetings too. I didn't think I'd be attending so many meetings when I got back, but somehow that's all I've managed to do. I haven't even made a single sketch yet. It's from one conference room to the next. And then the paperwork after."

Grant hums. "What about the restaurants you were going to design?"

I groan as I remember the meeting. "It was horrible because they didn't have any idea regarding what they wanted, and they disagreed with whatever we came up with. They disagreed with every single thing we said and left with no progress. We didn't even get to see the site today."

"Maybe give them a questionnaire to fill out, it helps at the garage when someone wants to change the color of their car but has no idea which color to go for."

I sigh. "We gave them one today, Edward's idea. You both think alike, actually. Hopefully, something good will come out of it, and they'll be able to tell us exactly what they'd like, or something close to it. This would be a great opportunity."

Grant hums again and goes quiet. It's not an uncomfortable silence; I'm starting to get used to it where we can just exist comfortably between ourselves. A silence where neither of us is desperate to say anything, and I find that it fills me with warmth more than anything.

We stay like that for a while, then Grant says, "Hey Wildflower, guess where I am?"

My heart stutters and then halts. I wonder if Grant knows what it does to me when he says that nickname in his low voice. I let out a sigh and settle further into my bed, ignoring the sound of my sheets rustling in favor of picking up sounds from his side of the phone.

But all I can hear is the whirling of my AC, the honking of cars outside, conversations of people making their way home. It frustrates me even more, being here in the city, back to the life that I spent so long trying to run away from.

"I'm at the fields, sitting under our tree and missing you."

My heart squeezes tightly and I have to force myself to breathe. I imagine the cool air blowing through my clothes and hair, the stars in the sky that I can never see in the city.

I think of the clear air that is replaced by all these fumes and the quiet I never manage to enjoy here. Everyone here is so busy that even the early mornings have someone moving around.

It's a whole routine to keep my sanity in this place, while Willow Falls offers me that comfort, even when I don't know I'm missing it.

Why did I think coming back to the city was worth it? Was it really that bad to fade into obscurity if it meant keeping my peace? And why was it fading into obscurity when I have a family I can rely on, a best friend who can give me all the support I need, and a man I love?

The realization that I love Grant doesn't stun me like it would have earlier. It feels like home, a soft melody in my ear that I finally have a name for.

A laugh escapes me.

"What's funny?" Grant asks, his voice light.

"I miss you so much, too," I say, but manage to hold myself from telling him just how much I miss him. If I'm going to tell him that I love him, I figure it will be best to do it in front of him. I need to return to Willow Falls.

Grant sighs, and I wonder why he was holding his breath. We return to our state of silence, and I fall asleep like I usually do during these calls with a smile on my face. Only this time, there's determination in my heart and a type of lightness on my shoulders.

I'm going to return home to Willow Falls.

This time, for good.

Chapter Twenty-Four

"You've got to be joking," Greg Jr. says, his voice loud and angry. His fists slam on his desk.

I flinch, but I don't bother taking my words back. My resignation letter is on the table, and my hands are folded behind my back to show respect. I didn't want to make a big deal out of this, but Greg Jr. is determined to do that for me.

"I'm sorry for getting everyone's hopes up, I genuinely thought I would be able to work here, but the longer I'm here, the more I feel out of place."

"You feel out of place? Do you know how much we're spending to have you here? Do you know how many loops we've jumped to get you back here? You think you're something special? How many places do you think will offer you close to what we're offering you, Alexis?"

"I understand and appreciate the belief you all have in me, but I can't be here any longer. I'd like to return to my hometown, and unlike the last time, I want to leave the right way. Plus, you failed to disclose my probation period and Edward. You planned for me to fail before I even started."

Greg Jr. scoffs and rounds the table to stand in front of me. Samuel and Edward draw closer like they intend to hold Greg Jr. back if he tries to attack me. I don't bother moving back or cowering. Greg Jr. is a lot of things, but he does have a good handle on his anger, even if he doesn't act like it.

I know how much the company and his father's approval mean to him. He won't throw all of that in the wind just because I decided to quit.

"I want you to know something, Alexis," Greg Jr. says right in my face, "we chased after you once before, but that won't happen again. If you walk out of this office without taking this resignation letter, that's it. All the graces you've enjoyed while working here will be stripped away. I won't let my father send Samuel after you anymore. There'll be no phone calls from me, no emails asking you to come back. No one will hire you."

I nearly danced in relief. It's all the indication I need to know that I'm serious about leaving this place.

"I understand that, and I want you to know that I don't take the opportunity you've given me lightly. If I could stay—"

"Get out," he cuts me off, voice firm, leaving no room for me to drop whatever comment is hanging on my lips.

I don't need to be told twice. I step out of the room and manage to keep my head high as I leave his office. Edward is hot on my tail. The second my door is closed, he starts pacing.

I didn't peg him to be a pacer.

"You'll be fine," I say to him as I pack my items in the box I got from the storage room before heading to see Greg Jr.

Edward scoffs as if the idea of me thinking he'll be anything but that is laughable. "I think you should worry about yourself right now. What are you going to do? He all but threatened to block you everywhere. What if you can't get a job?"

I tilt my head to the side. I had assumed that the threat was my imagination, but if Edward reached the same conclusion, then maybe I have something to worry about.

"He can't do that, I think," I say and shake my head. "It doesn't matter right now. I think it went better than I thought it would."

Edward scoffs again.

There's a knock on the door that interrupts what he's going to say next. Samuel steps into the office but doesn't bother coming all the way in after the door is shut.

"I'd like to not give the idea that I'm in cahoots with whatever madness possessed you," Samuel says, and turning to Edward, he adds, "I thought you'd know that too."

Edward doesn't need to be told twice; he spins on his heels and walks out of my office.

"I guess you finally read your email," Samuel says and nods his head in approval.

"My email? What do you mean?"

Samuel frowns. "You didn't read the email? So, you didn't see the... Why the hell are you quitting then?"

I open my mouth to say something, but Samuel holds his hand up to stop me. "I've been directed to let you know that you have three minutes to exit the premises, or security will be called in. You silly girl. What are you even doing?"

He spins around and steps out of the office, slamming the door on his way out. I see Greg Jr. look impossible and pleased by this action.

I just smile.

Much like the first time I left the city to go back to Willow Falls, I don't call home to let anyone know I'm coming back. But what's different this time is, I actually do call up the movers and tell them to get my things. I settled things with the building manager and left without worry.

The drive back this time is better, I feel lighter, like the weight of the world has been taken off my shoulders. I'm glad I got to come back to the city and make this decision. Staying in Willow Falls without making it out here and knowing for sure that I'm not going to enjoy it would have killed me.

When I drive past the garage, it's locked, but it doesn't matter. I know for a fact that I'll see Grant when I get back to the house. I try to picture him, where he is and what he's doing. He's going to be shocked to see me, but that will be nothing compared to my parents. Especially since I just spoke to them before I started the drive back.

I chuckle to myself. The last time I was making this drive, I was terrified and hoping the town would be enough to heal me. And now, I'm returning because I realize it did heal me and that I couldn't stay away any longer. In Willow Falls, I can start something small and convince someone to give me a chance. I can absolutely make it work this time around.

I roll down to the house and park in front beside my father's truck. I step out of my car, taking time to get my things out of the trunk. By the time I get the luggage out, enough time has passed for my parents to notice my arrival and rush out of the house.

My mother wobbles out, and they stand for a couple of seconds staring at me, and it occurs to me that the last time I was here, I broke down into tears.

"I quit my job," I say and smile at my parents, "for good this time!" I hope they can see how excited I am for this. My mother is the first one who moves, taking a tentative step towards me, waiting for a repeat performance, but I don't bother with it.

I smile wider and hug her tightly. "I'm so happy to be back home, you have no idea."

My mother chuckles lightly. "I was gearing up to comfort you again. What brought about this change?"

I pull back from the hug and go to my father to offer him a hug of his own. "You can say I came to my senses. Is Grant still here?"

"Oh honey, I'm sorry. Grant left town yesterday."

Chapter Twenty-Five

Acknowledgements

I would like to thank my fiancé, Johnny—this book exists because of you. Your patience, persistence and dreams are my dreams too. The field is ours to grow, and this is just the beginning. Thank you for believing in me and sharing the excitement of this new journey. To my two amazing kids and my family, thank you for your love, your understanding, and the little reminders that stories matter. You are my heart in every chapter.

To my editor, Danielle—thank you for guiding my words with such care and helping shape my story into something I am proud of. To Jessica and Lindsay, my talented graphic artists, thank you for bringing my vision to life in ways I couldn't have imagined. To my biggest supporters, you know who you are—thank you for keeping my secret safe until I was ready to share it with the world. Your excitement gave me courage .To my Beta team—CM, Gina, Vickie, Kim, Lindsay, and April—you each played such an important part in shaping this book. Thank you for your honesty, your enthusiasm, and the time you dedicated to helping me grow Wildflower Summer into its best version.

A heartfelt thank you to the indie authors who welcomed me with open arms and offered guidance when I needed it most. Your kindness and generosity reminded me why this community is so special. And to my ARC readers—thank you for taking an early leap with me. Your feedback, passion, and support mean more than you know. Thank you for believing in me, for cheering me on, and for being a part of this journey.

Stick around for more of Alexis and Grant's story.

About the author

Alyssa lives in a small midwest town, where she balances her full-time career as a registered nurse and her passion for storytelling. When she's not working or writing she is enjoying time with her two boys and amazing fiancé who's unwavering support fuels her love for books and life. Alyssa also has an obscured number of chickens whom she loves very much. Surrounded by the chaos and joy of family life, Alyssa finds inspiration in everyday moments and believes there's a story waiting to be told in the quietest corners of small-town life.

You can find me on Tiktok and IG
@AlyssaJ_writer

www.ingramcontent.com/pod-product-compliance
Lightning Source LLC
Chambersburg PA
CBHW070514160726
48003CB00004B/1562